# OPERATION
# SEA LION

Edited by Richard Cox

# Operation
# Sea Lion

PRESIDIO PRESS
SAN RAFAEL · CALIFORNIA

Published in 1977 by
PRESIDIO PRESS
1114 Irwin Street
San Rafael, California 94901


First published in Great Britain by Thornton Cox Limited, January 1975
Introduction and narrative © Richard Cox 1974
Article "The War Lords" © Alan Clark 1974
Other articles © *Daily Telegraph Limited* 1974

Library of Congress Catalog Card Number 74-21513
ISBN 0-89141-015-5


Printed in the United States of America

# Contents

TO

Tom Hawkyard, who first thought of it, John Anstey,
Christopher Angeloglou, Gill Carswell and Rosamund Man,
of the *Daily Telegraph Magazine*; to Christine Chambers who
typed it; and to Mance with love

My thanks are also due to the large number of people who
co-operated in the research on this book and on the preparation
of the War Game held at the Royal Military Academy,
Sandhurst. I particularly want to thank Admiral Doctor
Schunemann of the German Embassy, Admiral Ruge, General
Adolf Galland, General Heinz Trettner, Professor Doctor
Jürgen Rohwer of the Bibliothek Für Zeitgeschichte in
Stuttgart and the Curator of the Intelligence Corps Museum.
The research done by Mr Paddy Griffith and Commander
Thomas at the Royal Military Academy and the help of Mr
David Chandler and Mr Anthony Brett-James was also
invaluable.

Finally, I must acknowledge the extent to which I have drawn
on the excellent book by Mr Walter Ansell entitled 'Hitler
Confronts England', published by the Duke University Press,
Durham, USA in 1960.

The publishers would like to thank the following for permission
to reproduce the illustrations appearing in this book:

General Adolf Galland: 1; Admiral Ruge: 2a; Brian Kirley:
2b; Bibliothek für Zeitgeschichte: 3a, 3b; The Imperial War
Museum: 5, 6a, 6b, 7a, 7b, 8a, 9a, 9b, 13a; Keystone Press
Agency: 8b; Bundesarchiv: 10a, 10b, 11a, 11b, 12a, 12b, 14a,
15a, 15b, 16a; Robert Hunt Library: 13b, 16b.

Royal Navy

**U Boats**

...... *OKH Initial Bridgehead*

— — — *1st OKH Operational Objective*

—·—·— *2nd OKH Operational Objective*

(OKH—Oberkommando des Herres
—Army High Command)

The 1st Operational Objective was
to be reached in 10 days.

Orkney Isles

**Home Fleet**
Pentland Firth
*Scapa Flow*

Rosyth

**Home Fleet**

Hartlepool

*Humber*

E A S T
A N G L I A

Milford Haven

Severn

Malden

**Home Fleet**

Oxford

**London**

*Thames Estuary*

Chatham

Southampton
Bournemouth

Portsmouth

Hythe

*Goodwin
Sands*

Dunkirk

Ostend

Dover

B E L G I U M

Brighton

Hastings
Boulogne

Calais

Plymouth

*Lyme Bay*

**Isle of Wight**

Etaples

**16**
**Armee**

Scilly Isles

Cherbourg

Dieppe

Le Havre

**9**
**Armee**

F R A N C E

**6**

卐 **Army Group A**

# Foreword

The German paratroops jumped at dawn, as they had done in Holland, in Belgium, in Norway. But this time there were more of them. Nearly 8,000 *Fallschirmjäger* of the Seventh Flieger division, carried by a stream of 600 Junkers 52 transports, ugly three-engined beasts, flying a bare 150 feet above the Channel to stay below the British radar and only pulling up to their 400-foot dropping height as they crossed the Kentish coast at Hythe. The time was six o'clock on the morning of September 22, 1940, just a few minutes after official sunrise on a grey, cloudy, windless day. Below the long lines of aircraft the unwontedly calm sea was dark with the countless barges and motor boats of the invasion fleet. By breakfast time close on 90,000 troops were successfully ashore on beaches between Folkestone and Seaford. *Sealion* Day had begun.

Fiction? Of course. But strongly factual. This was precisely how the German High Command planned *Sealion*. They aimed to capture most of southern England within ten days. They would launch *Sealion* between September 19 and 26, when the tides would be right. On September 15 Hitler postponed the plan until 1941 and it died, as his soldiers died in the snows of Russia. Had he stuck to *Sealion*, would he have succeeded? The question has fascinated a generation of military writers. What follows in this book is a narrative account of the battle based on a War Game organised by *The Daily Telegraph Magazine* and the Department of War Studies at the Royal Military Academy, Sandhurst, in a carefully planned effort to determine the answer.

The game was actually held in the Staff College, close to Sandhurst, under the sponsorship of the Commandants of both these renowned establishments. A panel of German umpires, all of general's rank, flew in from Germany. So did the ex-Luftwaffe officer "playing" Goering, and Professor Rohwer, Director of the Institute of Defence Research in Stuttgart, who took the naval role. The German army "player" was Colonel Wachsmutt, then the Bundeswehr liaison officer at the Staff

7

College. The Germans were supported by their Defence Attaché in London, Admiral Schunemann. It was an impressive array of military expertise, and the British were no less well represented, with the backing of the Ministry of Defence.

The *Kriegspiel*, or War Game, is a Prussian invention, and a highly practical one at that. Early in 1940 the German High Command did a Game on their projected invasion of France – and then obeyed its lessons in the real attack of May, 1940, with triumphant success. No Game was done on *Sealion*, though aspects of it were examined.

The scenario of our *Sealion* Game started with the known plans of each side. German and British officers played the respective German and British naval, army and air commanders, with Hitler and Churchill also represented. Each side had a command room at the Staff College from which decisions were telephoned to the main room and shown as moves on a large landscape model of South Eastern England and the Channel, specially made at the School of Infantry and laid out at the Staff College. The resultant battles were umpired by a panel of generals, admirals and air marshals, with disputes over exact losses settled by cutting cards – the traditional way – under the direction of the organiser, Paddy Griffith, a young War Studies lecturer at the Royal Military Academy.

Furthermore we obtained hitherto unpublished Admiralty records of the actual weather in the period September 19-30, 1940. It proved to have been initially more favourable to invasion than the long range forecasts which helped to dissuade Hitler and which historians invariably quote.

The panel of umpires was uniquely qualified, two for each service. There was General Adolf Galland, the Luftwaffe ace who in the autumn of 1940 was commanding a wing of ME 109 fighters on the French coast, who was a General at 31 and of whom Douglas Bader wrote: 'By any criterion, Galland is a brave man.' The British air umpire was Air Chief Marshal Sir Christopher Foxley-Norris, also much decorated, though quick-wittedly self-deprecating. 'No one could dispute my Battle of Britain record,' he remarked. 'It was love-two. I was shot

8

down twice.' The naval umpires were Admiral Friedrich Ruge, in 1940 Commodore of the *Kriegsmarine's* minesweeping flottila in the Channel and involved in the day to day *Sealion* preparations; and Rear Admiral Edward Gueritz, a Royal Navy amphibious warfare expert. Finally, the German army umpire was General Heinx Trettner, postwar Inspector General of the Bundeswehr and in 1940 on the staff of General Student, the German airborne Commander. His opposite number was a brisk moustachioed British paratroop officer, Major General Glyn Gilbert, the present Commandant of the Joint Warfare Establishment, who in September, 1940 was "a second lieutenant defending the end of Brighton pier'. It says much for the authenticity of the War Game that these six umpires agreed unanimously on the final outcome.

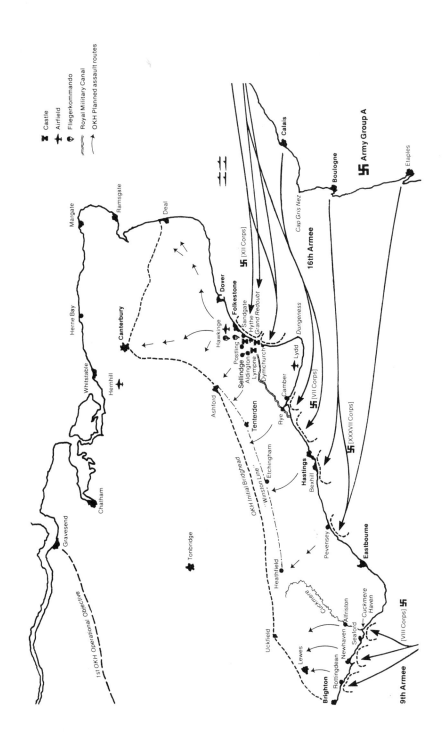

**Legend:**
- ♜ Castle
- ✈ Airfield
- ⊕ Fliegerkommando
- ⌇ Royal Military Canal
- → OKH Planned assault routes

1st OKH Operational Objective

Gravesend
Chatham
Whitstable
Herne Bay
Margate
Ramsgate
Deal

Hernhill
**Canterbury**
**Dover**

Tonbridge

Ashford
**Folkestone**
Hawkinge
Postling
Sellindge
Aldington
Lympne
Dymchurch
Sandgate
Hythe
*Grand Redoubt*
[XII Corps]

Tenterden
Etchingham
Winston Line
OKH Initial Bridgehead

Rye
Camber
Lydd
*Dungeness*
[VII Corps]

Uckfield
Lewes
Heathfield
**Hastings**
Bexhill
[XXXVII Corps]

**Brighton**
Rottingdean
Newhaven
Seaford
Alfriston
Cuckmere
Cuckmere Haven
Pevensey
**Eastbourne**

[VIII Corps]
**9th Armee**

Calais
Boulogne
Etaples
Cap Gris Nez
**Army Group A**
**16th Armee**

# Chapter One

*Sealion Hour - Dawn - September 22nd 1940*

The spirit stove flickered, spat, then began to heat the battered tin kettle with a steady flame. The bombardier crouched by it on the stone floor, his thin body casting a grotesque shadow on the walls. He shivered. It was cold, bloody cold for September. But what else would it be in the east tower of a medieval castle half an hour before dawn with shreds of fog swirling over the Romney Marsh below? Bombardier Brown wondered if it was true that the ghost of a Roman soldier walked the battlements, as the old gardener said. But the gardener also said the castle had been modernised – in 1360. Very funny. Brown shivered again, uneasily.

'Tea's up, Sir', he called out a few minutes later and handed a mug to the lieutenant standing by the window. The lieutenant groped and then took it without looking round. His eyes were attuned to the dark and he didn't want to lose night vision. As a Forward Observation Officer for the few coast guns there were between Folkestone and Dymchurch he had only two aids – his own precious pair of Zeiss binoculars and that other pair of what his idiot commanding officer persisted in calling 'the mark one human eyeball.' From this tower of Lympne Castle, apparently, you could see the lights of cars in France of a clear night. In peacetime. But this was the early morning of Sunday, September 22nd 1940 and what worried the Lieutenant was that for an hour he'd been seeing flashes of light out to sea. A few shells had fallen in Hythe. That hardly explained the flashes. The Lieutenant wondered just how noticeable this Observation Post was from the air. It was cleverly built out of the roof of the tower, its long narrow window surmounted by fake battlements, even a fake chimney. The castle stood just beneath the top of a long escarpment, at the foot of which ran the wide Royal Military Canal, constructed as a defence against Napoleon in 1804. From down there the OP was scarcely visible, largely hidden by trees.

11

Nor had the castle been attacked in any of the dive bomber raids on Lympne airfield, directly behind it. Those raids were so bad that after the Navy Skua squadron left in May the airfield ceased to be used. Maybe the OP could not been seen. The Lieutenant remembered the gardener telling them how Lympne Castle had been requisitioned every time invasion threatened, when the Dutch fleet massed in 1667; when the Martello Towers by the beach and the canal were being built to resist Napoleon; in the Great War. There was still a drawing on the tower door of the devil, red-bodied, blue-tailed and wearing a yellow spiked pickelhaube helmet. If the Hun did his homework he'd know Lympne Castle would be in military use again.

Lieutenant Pearson-Smith was an over age, even slightly paunchy, emergency subaltern of 36, who had read history at Oxford. He remembered the few German undergraduates who were his contemporaries as being almost unbearably thorough and took it for granted that the German General staff would have studied both Caesar's and Napoleon's invasion plans. There'd been a Roman Camp on this hill, and a Saxon one. That fifteen mile stretch of sand and shingle between Sandgate and Dungeness was an obvious landing place, even though it was now obstructed by stands of scaffolding, hung with mines and booby traps.

With a dull crash the two guns in the castle gardens fired. The tower shook.

'The Newfoundlanders' famous infra-red must have picked up something,' commented Pearson-Smith. Ironically the fiercely independent Newfoundland Regiment had deployed two of their antique twenty mile range Great War mark 19 six inch guns here. They were controlled by an FOO miles away beyond Dymchurch, with the aid of a highly secret infra-red searchlight, while Pearson-Smith's battery was back in the countryside near Aldington dependent on his binoculars.

'Bloody typical' Brown had called it.

'See anything, Sir?' The bombardier asked.

'Only the gunfire. I suppose it's gunfire. What time is it, Brown?'

12

'Five thirty two, Sir. Sunrise five forty five, according to the tables.'

'It's this damn cloud.'

Outside the cloud was a low dark blanket overhead, drifting slowly in from the south, seeming to hold off the dawn. But already the long curve of the shore was visible in the grey light, and the fog patches in the marsh showed whiter. A little rain spattered the window.

Suddenly the whole surface of the sea came alive with needles of light, while tiny flowers of flame blossomed on the shore, to be instantly extinguished in smoke. As the two watched, momentarily fascinated, the creeping dawn light revealed a huge flotilla of barges that stretched across the whole sweep of Dymchurch Bay, moving in at infinitesimal speed. Ahead of them surged dozens of motorboats, racing to the beach, along which billowing smoke began to drift. Then, coming steadily nearer and more urgent, they heard the throbbing drone of aircraft engines. Not tens but hundreds, many hundreds.

Pearson-Smith seized the radio microphone lying on the window ledge, and almost choking, shouted his opening order to the guns.

'Regimental target. HE Airburst.'

Distantly, despite the crackling static he could hear the responding roar to the gunners 'Take Post.' Then he handed the microphone to Brown and hurriedly began taking bearings with a compass. The din from the aircraft was intense. But, he realised, they were passing across his front, towards Hythe and Saltwood, not directly overhead.

Sergeant Wyall of the Home Guard in Hythe, snatching two hours sleep after a night's duty, was woken by the noise. He was in his late fifties now, still bull-like and strong – he'd been a heavy weight boxer in his twenties – but he got tired these days. Pulling his scratchy new battledress trousers on over his pyjamas, he ran out of the side door of his terraced cottage and down the cracked cement path to the road, where he could get a clear view. A crackle of machine gun fire came from the sea front. He took no

13

notice. His eyes were on the sky..Until now it had been bombers and fighters over Hythe; Heinkel IIIs, Messerschmitts and the 'flying pencil' Dornier 17s, heading for London or jettisoning their bombs on the way back as they retreated from the Spitfires and Hurricanes of the RAF. These aircraft were strangers. Then he remembered the Junkers 52 from the recognition pamphlet. Its three engines were unmistakable. 'Carries twelve to eighteen troops, fully equipped' – paratroops.

'Christ,' he muttered to himself, 'if they drop on the hill and come back down, they'll slaughter us.'

There were only three hundred Home Guards in Hythe and not all of them had rifles yet. The regulars on the seafront had only just got theirs, such had been the losses at Dunkirk.

'I must get the platoon onto the Nelson's Head bridge, double quick,' he thought.

The bridge was one of the two left across the Military Canal. The third had been dismantled to make the canal less easy for an invader to cross. As Sergeant Wyall ran back indoors to finish dressing, the guns on the seafront opened up point blank at the barges coming in on the calm dark sea. Shells began to explode in the town, dogs howled and children woke and cried.

The pilot of the leading Junkers had found Hythe easily, despite the night flight and the low cloud. From his base at Lille the 113 kilometers to Cap Gris Nez had taken forty one minutes and with only a whisper of a southerly wind the dim outline of the English coast came in sight fourteen minutes after that. He scarcely saw the vast fleet invasion barges beneath, though the flicker of gunfire suggested trouble. His formation carried Oberst Meindl's battalion, one of the best in the Seventh Fliegerdivision. Meindl himself crouched behind him in the cockpit. Immediately they saw the coast the pilot ordered "Action Stations" on the intercom and concentrated on the route he had learnt from the reconnaisance photos, turning on to the final heading of 320 degrees two kilometres or so from the shore. Behind him fifty more 'Tante Ju's' followed suit. They should run in over a big white hotel on the Hythe seafront. There it was. 'On track, two kilometres,' he yelled to Meindl, who nodded and darted back to hook up. Meindl always jumped first. A burst of tracer came up from close to the hotel. No matter. Hold steady. Down to 150 metres, throttle back. Hold steady. Red light on – he flipped the switch.

Back in the noise of engines and slipstream the Absetzer saw the light, roared out 'Fertig zum Sprung'. Meindl, a smallish though broad shouldered man, crouched in the low door, bracing himself on the side handles in the roar of the slipstream. The klaxon shrieked even louder. He launched himself out, spreadeagled. Look up, chute open. Gut. Look round. There were the towers of Saltwood Castle. Trees everywhere. Twenty seconds later and the ground was coming up at him. Legs apart. Fall forward. Oberst Meindl hit the ploughed field, and rolled over, the first invader on English soil since the Dutch in 1667. Above, the lightening sky was dense with parachutes. The time was 0547, Sealion Hour plus two minutes.

Two miles further inland Oberst Brauer's battalions were tumbling out of their Junkers 52s between Paddlesworth and Etchinghill villages, their objective the heights above Sandgate, where the medieval Pilgrims Way winds along the escarpment towards Canterbury.

At S plus 65, as the infantry were still swarming out of their barges on the Hythe and Dymchurch beaches, the rest of the 7th Fliegerdivision dropped round Sellindge and Postling to secure the outer perimeter of the bridgehead and to take Lympne airfield. By S plus 90 there were all but 8,000 paratroops in that corner of Kent, trampling the hop fields and the fallen leaves. By nightfall they hoped to be in Folkestone, and after that, Dover.

Simultaneously beaches were being stormed at Dungeness, at Cuckmerehaven and at Newhaven. When Hitler had finally decided on September 15th to confirm his Generals' invasion plan he let loose an armada that would eventually total no less than 330,000 men, the first three days seeing the vast but exact total of 110,167 men and 24,528 horses ashore. That is if none were lost at sea. Much of the artillery was still horse drawn.

As the assault went in Generaloberst Ernst Busch, com-

15

mander of the 16th Army, stood in his heavy field grey greatcoat before the map tables in a requisitioned *lycee* in Calais. Even indoors he could hear the drone of aircraft. What he listened calmly for was the first crackling radio message from the English beaches. Busch was a thoroughly professional soldier. That was why, though by no means the ultimate Sealion commander, the practical responsibility for the operation had fallen on his shoulders. Now, after the weeks of intense planning, he had reached the moment no general can escape, the moment when the troops have gone over the top and he can only wait for the news on which to base the next decision. He had deliberately chosen to spend that long night of waiting among his men in their Calais assembly area, rather than back in the comfort of the country house near Lille that was his headquarters. His Chief of Staff, General Model, was there. Model could cope.

A corporal put a cup of coffee down on the trestle table. Busch sipped and reflected. Sealion had already had its ups and downs. His own superior, Feldmarschall Gerd von Rundstedt, had little faith in it. That was why Busch had signed the final orders on his behalf eight days ago, a bare twenty four hours after that extraordinary lunch which the Supreme Commander, the Führer himself, had given for the Colonel Generals on September 13th. It had been a gala occasion. He and nineteen others, all newly promoted, had been invited to pay respects to their Leader. He in turn had been genial and relaxed. He'd particularly wanted to talk to Busch and to the other army commander Generaloberst Strauss about Sealion. Busch had expected high sounding reiteration of the phrases in the August 30th directive that had put Sealion into top gear.

'The mighty landing in England' it said, had for its aim 'to eliminate the English homeland as a base for continuing the war against Germany and if the need develops, occupy it completely.' To Busch's acute surprise the Führer told them that in the current favourable air situation he had 'no thought of accepting too great a risk as was posed by a landing in England.' And the Führer declared this with the most disarming frankness. Busch was used to concealing his emotions. His strong thickly fleshed face showed no trace of the astonishment he felt. During the flight back to Lille, however, he tried furiously to reason out the Führer's true intentions. Of course there was a caution in the phrasing of that original order, a caution about the need to occupy England that echoed the Führer's often avowed belief that England would see reason and capitulate now that France had fallen and that the Luftwaffe was daily bombing English cities. The Führer's enormous faith in Reichsmarschall Goering's Luftwaffe was also well known. But what in the name of all the Gods should he, Busch, tell his troops, the soldiers for whose crossing two thousand barges had been assembled in the Channel ports and whose landing practices he had watched on the once fashionable Le Touquet beaches? Their morale was at its peak. Loudspeakers constantly blared forth the song 'Wir fahren gegen Engelland' in their camps. What should he tell them?

Unexpectedly the answer had come the very next morning. The Führer ordered Sealion into action at the first possible date. That meant between September 19th and 26th when dawn would coincide with the Navy's requirement of a landing two hours or so after high tide. So Busch that day signed the order, reckoning it would take eight days to gain the first operational objective, all of Kent, Surrey, Sussex and Hampshire that lay within a line from the Thames Estuary, along the heights south of London and down to Portsmouth.

The remnant of the coffee grew cold as Busch waited for the radio message. In fact the first news came at 0557 from the Air Fleet Third Headquarters on neighbouring French soil and it came by telephone – a laconic signal 'Initial Sealion parachute drop completed on schedule. Reichsmarschall Goering informed.' That meant the Führer informed. The Luftwaffe lost no opportunity for earning itself plaudits, Busch reflected irritably.

Another hour passed before a radio operator, crouching in the lee of a sand dune on the Hythe rifle ranges, tapped out a situation report in morse from his unit. 'Fifty-fifth regiment advance detachment landed. Storming Grand Redoubt to establish firebase. Commanding Officer wounded.' Hardly a perfect

17

report, thought Busch, snapping out, 'Tell them to transmit every half hour', before reaching for the direct line to von Rundstedt's headquarters at the villa near Paris. 'Busch here. Generaloberst Busch. Yes, fetch him.' He waited briefly. Perhaps this news would persuade von Rundstedt to stop talking about 'Sealion rubbish' and take more of an interest. 'Busch speaking Herr Feldmarschall. The first echelon has landed successfully. At least of Loch's Division. I expect reports from the others shortly. They're not called the Sturmbock for nothing. Yes, the first detachments of Fallschirmjäger have landed. We should be in Folkestone tonight. Yes, Feldmarschall. Heil Hitler'. He rang off. Now, of course, von Rundstedt wanted results. No longer was Sealion an unwelcome vision of the Führer's, which with luck would be abandoned. Now it was up to the professionals to make it work. If it failed, all their heads would roll together. But it would not fail. The detailed planning, despite the bare six weeks allowed for it, had been meticulous. The moves had been drilled exhaustively. Above all, the men were on the top of their form after the fantastic victory in France. They were well trained, well armed, fit and in the mood to conquer the world, a world in which England stood alone.

What General Busch did not yet know, and Lieutenant Pearson-Smith peering at pinpricks of light out to sea from his eyrie in Lympne Castle had only guessed at, was that the massive night crossing had met with unexpected opposition. Though the invasion fleet had sailed at dusk, making air observation difficult, an armed British trawler had bumped the long lines of barges early. Her captain's radio report, made even as an E-boat sank her with all hands, had been picked up at Dover. By midnight the Admiralty had ordered the Home Fleet to sail south at full steam from Scapa Flow and Rosyth, which they did by 0200, to be promptly ambushed by waiting U-boats. But in any case it would be twenty four hours or more before they were in action in the Channel. What were available immediately were motor torpedo boats, the Royal Navy's equivalent to the German E-boats and S-boats, sleek fast grey painted killers, the joy of the lieutenants who commanded them. Moreover they were based in Dover, already inside the screen of mines that Commodore Ruge's two hundred assorted mine and picket vessels had been laying for the past eight days to protect the flanks of the invasion sealanes, ten rows of mines each one hundred metres apart in every one of four long minefields. At the Channel's eastern end, minefield 'Caesar' off the Goodwin Sands, guarded the lane from Ostend and Dunkirk invasion beach 'B' between Hythe and Dymchurch. Along this route a vast procession of steamers, barges and small craft had to pass, not merely once, but back and forth over a period of weeks to bring in supplies, though the next few days would be the crucial ones.

'But the mines will not stop all British ships' Ruge had warned 'Some always get through'.

The MTBs, racing across a calm sea with surface visibility good beneath the cloud, made contact at 0235.

A tug captain saw them first, or rather saw the ghostly white spume of their wake. He thought they were E-boats shepherding the ungainly herd onto the correct course. 'The pigpile', as Ruge used rudely to refer to it. His tug was one of six, each towing two barges in tandem. Behind him the cable alternately dipped and tautened with the swell. Behind that rode another. They were Rhine grain barges both and the seventy men crammed alongside four trucks in the hold of each knew it well from the chaff and dust that blew from every crevice. And they were deep these barges. The soldiers, trying to doze, propped against their equipment, heads lolling on their life-jackets, queasy despite the issue sickness pills they'd taken at Dunkirk, could see nothing. Even the Petty Officers, up in the wheelhouse, had no communication with the tug captain except by megaphone, nor he with them.

When the captain saw the spray from the salvo of torpedoes and realised, incredulously, that he was under attack, that what he had taken for E-boats were in fact enemy, there was no way he could warn the barges. By instinct he wrenched the tug's wheel hard to port. Even as the helm began to answer sluggishly, machine gun bullets cracked into the wheelhouse, splintering the planks, and the salvo burst against the second craft. Its starboard side collapsed and the whole hulk was thrown up out of the water, to fall back broken. The vehicles slid around, crushing men's bodies as the sea gushed in. In less than a minute it had sunk, mercifully snapping the tow cable, though rocking and dragging the leading barge so violently that the tug captain feared they would all go down together.

Then, just as rapidly, all was over. Only the bursts of flame showed where other boats were being hit. The tug captain stared aft into the darkness, noticed the absence of a dark shadow where the lost barge had been, muttered a prayer and settled back to re-establish his course. His tug, the *Anne Marie*, had been doing its proper job up in Hamburg docks a mere month ago. Then he'd been ordered to Dunkirk for 'special duties' – towing two overladen canal barges across thirty miles of water notorious for its tides and gales. Special duty! Suicide more like.

He thought of those barges in their proper element, chugging gently down the Rhine, with gay print curtains in the windows of the tiny cabins at the stern, which the barge owner and his wife and their children called home, with the washing flapping on a clothes line and the vineyards and castles slipping past on the stretch between Bad Godesberg and Mainz. That was what they were built for. Peaceful days and shallow water. Now they had been hastily stripped, fitted with more powerful engines, some mounted with awkward platforms for flak guns, and expected to survive crossing the English Channel. If the seastate became worse than mild or the wind more than light they risked swamping and even so could average only three knots. By some miracle the bad long range weather forecast for this period had been wrong. The depression heading south east from Iceland had taken a turn to the north east and passed over Norway instead of Britain. It was the kind of miracle ordinary men with wives and families could manage without. All the captain of the *Anne Marie* could do now was make certain that he cast off the remaining barge well short of the beach, letting it ride in on its own power, and keeping the *Anne Marie* clear to get away again from the mêlée of the landing.

If the captain of the tug *Anne Marie* cherished a simple view of his own role, a view centred on survival, who can blame him? In the dark each tow could do no more than follow the next, the Leutnant leading each group of tows in a motorboat could only follow the group in front. Yet the 180 barges from the one port of Dunkirk had joined in a column with auxiliary minesweepers carrying six man sturmboote that would race in through the surf for the first assault, with steamers carrying supplies, with huge catamarans made of two pontoons joined by a platform on which flak guns were mounted, with coasters jury rigged with artillery to give further fire support to the landing. Then, in the dark and competing with a four knot tide, this unwieldy column from Dunkirk had tried to unite with another from Ostend to make the full force destined for beach 'B'. And finally, when ten miles out from the English shore, the combined column had to execute a right turn so that it would make the actual landing in line abreast. And for this manoeuvre only the leading ships had radios. Communication with the rest depended on verey lights and good old fashioned shouting through a megaphone. But that was the manoeuvre the Fleet Commander, Vize Admiral Lutjens, had ordered. After considering its implications the Kriegsmarine Commandant at Dunkirk, the stocky Captain Heinrich Bartels, had decided to take a motor-boat himself and personally direct the crossing to beach 'B'. The tug captain had heard about Bartels coming. It was the sort of detail that gave ordinary men more confidence.

Likewise Oberstleutnant Adolf Galland gave very personal leadership to his ME 109 wing, the JG 26. Its squadrons had recently moved to strips around Wissant, close by Cap Gris Nez where Kesselring had brought the advance Headquarters of his Second Air Fleet. The fields had been farms. Just as Galland ousted the cows to make room for his Messerschmitts, so he took over a farmhouse to make an officers' mess. It was as close to England as was physically possible on land. One of his 109s with a Mickey Mouse emblazoned on the fuselage below the cockpit, was over Kent almost more often than it was at home. He had two of his own, so one was always serviceable. On August 1st, Kesselring had decorated him with the Knights Cross, while photographs of the Reichsmarshall's subsequent visit occupied many fresh pages in the squadron scrapbook. There were Goering's two special trains, one for him, one for his staff; there he stood, his huge bulk resplendent in a white uniform, admiring the 'kills' marked up on the tail of Galland's aircraft. Goering wanted a lot out of his pilots this autumn and he liked to be on the spot when big operations began, even if he not infrequently issued orders from the comfort of his train through the improbable, though strong voiced medium of his personal nurse, Schwester Christa.

Finally, the Führer himself had come to inspect the huge concrete gun emplacements at Cap Gris Nez from which Dover would be bombarded ahead of the landings. He prided himself on his detailed knowledge of artillery and could quote the range and projectile weight of every piece the army possessed. These thirty monster guns in their fortresses distilled the reality of Sealion for him more than any plans or maps. Here his whole vast inspiration for defeating England took form and shape.

Nonetheless somewhere at some level between the Führer and the steel helmeted troopers, someone had to keep a minute by minute hold on the development of the operation. It could only be done beach by beach. That was why men like Captain Bartels were at each of the five main landing beaches. That was why the Commander of each of the nine Divisions was on board a small steamer with his staff, close behind the advance detachments and ready to take immediate control of his beachhead. As the fleet carrying the 17th Division, led by Bartel's motorboat, moved ponderously in wavering line abreast towards the Kentish shore, Generalmajor Herbert Loch stood on the bridge of his steamer. He was a thin man, Loch, whose narrow bespectacled face seemed dwarfed by the high hat with the General's gold cords above its shiny peak. But the Iron Crosses at his collar and on his left breast pocket, coupled with his other decorations bespoke a toughness that his appearance lacked. He and his Division had distinguished themselves in Poland and at the battles for Fortress Longwy and Chateau Porcien during the brief French campaign. Now, through binoculars, he was looking out for his first headquarters on English soil, that same big square white building on which the pilot of Meindl's aircraft would be lining up in a few minutes for his run into Saltwood. Loch knew the building's name as well as the Hythe Home Guard did. It was the Imperial Hotel.

'The hotel has recently changed hands,' remarked the Intelligence Officer standing by him on the bridge of the steamer.

'And is about to again,' said Loch.


The defenders of Hythe's long, gently shelving beaches were regulars, while Sergeant Wyall and three hundred others in the Home Guard were allotted to strong points in the town and along the Royal Military Canal. Not surprisingly the key fortifications on the seafront were those same thick walled Martello towers that had been built as a defence against Napoleon's expected invasion in 1804. They were now surmounted by hurriedly built concrete gunslits for machine gunners, while the monarch of them all, the huge moated Grand Redoubt, midway between Hythe and Dymchurch, boasted emplacements for six inch guns. Then to bolster the Martello Towers there were pillboxes on the sea wall and along the little roads and narrow waterways, 'main drains' as the locals called them – that intersect the Romney Marsh. It was a weak defence. Everyone knew the real fighting would take place back along the obstacle of the Military Canal at the foot of the escarpment behind the Marsh. But there was one hope. Not only was there a protective boom in the sea. All along the beach, just above the low water mark, were stands of builders' scaffolding, hung with explosive booby traps. These ought to tear the keels out of the incoming barges. And if they didn't, then the thousands of mines laid in the shingle ought to, while the crossfire of the machine gunners massacred the troops floundering in the water, and the six inch guns pumped shells into the boats at point blank range. So the men in the pillboxes held their fire as they watched the fleet on the horizon, waiting to 'see the whites of their eyes' in the old phrase.

Unexpectedly, smoke shells began to fall along the seafront, mixed with heavier fire from 174 mm artillery. The smoke drifted very slowly inland. Overhead Spitfires and Hurricanes, weaving in and out of the cloud to attack the boats in the dim dawn light, added to the gunners' confusion. Several of the paratroops Junkers 52s were shot down. One crashed on the little golf course by the Imperial Hotel setting off half a dozen of the Teller mines laid there, the funeral pyre of its wreckage raising a transitory column of thick black smoke. The noise was intense, with the hesitant bursts of machine gun fire from the defenders counter-pointing the howl of aircraft engines. Men crouched in improvised dugouts made of concrete drainpipe buried in the shingle, their Bren guns cocked and the safety catches off, waited tensely for the barges to grind into the hidden obstacles. A gunner in the Grand Redoubt complained.

'Christ, it's all bloody slow motion. And where's their artillery? In rowing boats I suppose.' The sergeant, the No. 1 on the gun, answered brusquely.

'This is the softening up bit. They'll be on the doorstep soon enough.' He looked at his watch. It was nine minutes past six.


At that moment Captain Bartels, five hundred yards out to sea in his motorboat, also checked the time. He made it ten seconds before 0610. The twenty minute bombardment was over. He pulled out a signal pistol, flicked the catch, glanced to see it was correctly loaded, and stretching his arm high up, fired. The blue flare curved towards the cloud, spat stars, fell back towards the sea like a party firework. Abruptly the artillery stopped. Cradles slung on the sides of minecraft and fishing cutters tilted to launch over a hundred stormboats, engines racing before they even hit the water. They were basic military speedboats specially designed for this assault and tested on similar beaches in France. In each, six men crouched ready to jump ashore. The seventh, the coxswain, would take the boat back for another load. The sea was only just on the ebb from high tide and with their shallow draught the stormboats passed clear over the unseen obstacles. The defenders, peering through the drifting acrid smoke, saw the boats coming head on, bows clear of the swell, and waited for the scaffolding to tear their keels out.

'Jesus,' cried the gunner, 'It's gone wrong.'

From his emplacement, a good twenty feet up, he could see the boats beaching all along the shore. The crouching men were out and sprinting through the surf before they even grounded. Showers of sand and pebbles cascaded up as a few mines detonated. Yet nothing stopped the tide of men sweeping up to the sea wall, firing from the hip and bayonets fixed. For the defenders in the drainpipes the end was quick and grisly. A few in pillboxes held out longer, until the flamethrowers were brought into action.

At the Grand Redoubt the gunner spotted what was obviously an officer rallying his men below, seized his rifle and more by luck than skill put a shot through his throat. It was Major Panwitz, commanding the advance detachment of the 55th Regiment. Thirty seconds later he was dying, as the blood pumped out of a severed artery on to the shingle.

This was when the signaller thirty yards away sent back the first message across the Channel, the message Busch in turn passed to von Rundstedt. And as Busch remarked, the 17th was not known as the Battering Ram division for nothing. Within five minutes an Unteroffizier standing right under the outer wall of the Redoubt where the gunners inside could not see him, succeeded in lobbing a grenade clear over the outer wall and the moat and into one of the gun emplacement openings, killing two of the crew and disabling the others. Five minutes after that two assault engineers were round the back of the Redoubt, laying a charge against the massive wooden outer door while others gave them covering fire. With the doors blown it was only a matter of time before the British gunners were overwhelmed in the rabbit warren of passages. By 0700 the guns were silent. Alongside their empty barrels the muzzles of German heavy machine guns pro-

25

truded from the concrete slits, covering the 55th's regrouping.

The barges with the rest of the advance detachment had equally come unscathed over the underwater scaffolding, though in their case because their great weight crushed it. So the dead Panwitz's 'Himmelfahrtskommando', the advance detachment command whose dangers 'guaranteed a ride to heaven', had all but 1200 men ashore, equipped and fighting. The Adjutant took command, briefly assembling the officers behind the Redoubt.

'As soon as the main boats are ashore we'll move five hundred metres down to the little railway. That's our forming up point for the assault. Remember General Loch's order "Clear the beach and drive for the heights". Now move!' Struck by a sudden thought he pointed to the escarpment and the low silhouette of Lympne Castle among the trees.

'Let's get to those canal bridges ahead of our friends, the paratroops, up there.'

Much of the same happened with the landing at Hythe, except that the 21st Regiment met more intense opposition. The regulars held on grimly, especially at the Imperial Hotel, surrounded as it was by slit trenches and anti aircraft guns. Indeed the combination of machine gun fire with mines and booby traps everywhere – on the ranges, the golf course, in car parks – held the Germans along the line of seafront hotels. Eight hundred yards back, at the Nelson's Head bridge, Sergeant Wyall and his Home Guard platoon, were dispersed on the steep banks of the canal.

'Our job,' he told them 'is to keep this bridge open for our own boys to get back across, right to the last minute. And when that moment comes, I blow the charges.'

The explosives had been laid under the arch many weeks ago by the Sappers. Sergeant Wyall ran the wires back to the wall of the Nelson's Head. When his platoon were clear he'd plunge the handle down and into the box and duck round the corner to escape the flying debris as the old brickwork went up. For the present there was constant traffic of men and vehicles across the bridge, including some horribly wounded men being brought back.

26

'Using flamethrowers, the bastards' he muttered to himself, as he saw one stretcher and its charred load pass.


Meanwhile, up at Saltwood on the wooded hill behind Hythe, Oberst Meindl had difficulty rallying his two battalions. Their dropping zone was a sloping field hemmed in by tall old trees and also divided in half by a line of trees. Men had landed in the branches and some of the vital fallschirmbomben were entangled. These were the equipment containers that held the MG 34 machine guns, with their unequalled nine hundred rounds per minute rate of fire; the light mortars and the men's carbines. The only weapons the troops carried on them were Schmeisser machine pistols and Lugers. When Meindl landed, he had his Schmeisser out of his smock and loaded within seconds of hitting the ground. That was the moment when you were most vulnerable, when you were freeing yourself from the parachute harness. But not a shot had been fired in opposition. Meindl hadn't paused to wonder why. Paratroop commanders seldom question the dispensations of Providence – they take advantage of them.

Meindl was first at the pre-arranged rallying point at the corner of the lower field, hidden only by hedges from the narrow road running down into Saltwood. As more men doubled in, he was giving orders.

'Hans, get two parties organised to recover those fallschirmbomben in the trees. No good waiting for the recovery party to assemble. And give them covering fire if they need it.'

He turned to the Adjutant. 'Kurt, get two platoons by the side of the road. Both battalions will move as planned in fifteen minutes.'

The Adjutant saluted. Meindl pulled a neatly folded map out of his smock pocket. It was a reprint of the 1939 edition of the local Automobile Association road map. He looked around. Extraordinary how from the air Saltwood Castle stuck out like a sore thumb, yet here, not five hundred yards away, it was invisible. Still, the cutting of the disused railway down into Hythe would conceal them from any British in the Castle, as well as

27

providing the quickest possible route down the hill by-passing the village. At this moment a Leutnant from the other battalion came running across for orders. Meindl wasted no words.

'Tell the Major we stick to the plan. I expect you on the canal west of Hythe within an hour. Move.'

The field was thick with men, the sooner they moved off the better. The Adjutant was back now.

'Should be ready in five minutes, Colonel,' he said adding 'Like Holland isn't it?'

Holland had been a walkover. Apparently the British believed they'd parachuted into Holland disguised as nuns. What nonsense. They'd have gone through the Dutch like butter if they'd been dressed in bathing suits. The British seemed equally unprepared on this Sunday morning.

'Don't be too sure,' cautioned Meindl.

'There are at least a thousand troops in Hythe and I want no unnecessary casualties.'

'Understood, Herr Oberst,' said the Adjutant, chastened.

Meindl was far from the popular image of a paratroop commander. Tough, yes. But careful for his men. He was as much a father to them as a leader, and it wasn't just because his age was almost fifty. Meindl genuinely cared for his soldiers. He appreciated the dash that some of them had shown in Holland and landing atop the fort of Eben Emael in Belgium. He also liked them to stay alive. At this moment, that meant setting his plans in action quickly and seizing the canal bridges before the British really woke up.

The Chatham and South East Railway used to bring enough visitors to Hythe for its owners to have invested in building the Railway Hotel, a bare half mile from the old station. After a royal visit it became, more grandly, The Imperial. Nonetheless the line lost money and was closed between the wars. But the cuttings dug by its Victorian engineers remained intact after the lines were taken up. They still led from the edge of Oberst Meindl's chosen dropping zone, under the Saltwood road, slantwise down a valley and into Hythe obligingly close to the canal bridge nearest to the hotel.

'Let's hope General Loch succeeds in keeping the chef,' said Meindl to his ADC as they checked section after section into the railway bed. Meindl was a Schwabian, a 'Cossack from the Danube', as they called them. He lacked the neighbouring Bavarians down-to-earth humour and his jokes were rare. The ADC laughed appropriately.

'We shall be hungry by lunchtime,' he replied, 'marching at this speed.'

The paratroops moved so fast that they were almost all off the dropping zone and out of sight down the cutting when the anti-paratroop platoon of the Green Howards, Tommy Guns in hand and laboriously pushing bicycles, came up the road from Saltwood. The NCO whom Meindl had detailed to guard the road bridge until everyone was clear could hardly believe his eyes. The English were either mad or incredibly incompetent. His men were well concealed in the hedge. He waited until he could hear one puffing cyclist say:

'They must have dropped up the top.'

Then he shouted 'Feuer'. It was a massacre. Only one Green Howard escaped, pedalling frantically down the hill again. The paratroops rose out of their concealment and, leaving the corpses in the road, plunged down the banks of the cutting to join the tail of the column.

That was the sole opposition encountered along the mile of railway bed, a mile they covered in a comfortable quarter of an hour. Then it was a mere six hundred yards to the canal bridge. Civilians were streaming up the road to leave the town, as rein-forcements marched down from St. Martin's Plain barracks. The paratroops' abrupt appearance caused panic, which they were well trained to exploit. As women shrieked and tried to hide in doorways, the Germans sprinted across the road, crouched on the corners and opened fire at the troops coming down, who broke ranks and dived for cover. A platoon that had already passed turned to make a stand at a garage, kneeling to shoot from behind the petrol pumps with their moulded glass tops. They could do little to stop the Germans fanning out and were swiftly overwhelmed. After that, as though by magic, the street

29

ahead was clear, with only an occasional sniper's bullet riccochetting on the paving stones. The bridge fell at 0712, its Home Guard defenders having been so completely taken by surprise that they failed to detonate the charges to blow it up. The few not killed were taken prisoner while the Germans occupied their slit trenches. Under Meindl's direction houses on both sides of the canal were broken into for use as machine gun posts. The inhabitants, women mostly, were herded with the Home Guard survivors into one building and told to keep quiet.

At 0740 a radio message from the other battalion informed Meindl that the canal bridge by the railway station had been captured. Since the Ladies Walk bridge had been dismantled as an anti-invasion precaution, there was now only one line of retreat for the British holding off the 17th Division on the seafront. That was the Nelson's Head bridge, held by Sergeant Wyall.

# Chapter Two

## *0800 to 1200   September 22nd*

St James's Park is familiar to most foreign visitors because Buckingham Palace stands magnificent at one end of it and the Horse Guards and Downing Street are at the other, while in between stretches a delightful lake on which live the royal collection of pelicans, Chinese duck and other exotic waterbirds. In 1939 the foreign visitors to the Park included a German couple clutching all the appropriate impedimenta of the serious tourist, and assiduously photographing everything from the charming Victorian iron bridge across the lake, to the array of Government buildings at the Horse Guards end. Particularly the Government buildings and Wellington Barracks. One of them spoke to the Park keeper and learnt that in the 1914-18 war the pelicans had suffered the indignity of removal. The lake had been drained for fear that the shining water would guide Zeppelin airships, which of course carried bombs, to Buckingham Palace. Subsequently temporary huts for civil servants were erected on the bed of the Lake. Back at their hotel in Victoria the tourists wrote all this down and in due course the information was filed away in the intelligence records of the Obercommando der Luftwaffe in Berlin.

In fact the 1914-18 precautions were not followed in 1940 and the Lake still showed up as clearly by both day and night as it did in the Luftwaffe's detailed aerial survey of Britain, the *Luftgeographisches Einzelheft Grossbritannien.*

On September 22nd, after breakfast, Luftwaffe staff officers were poring over this volume at the Obercommando building in Berlin.

'Here it is,' exclaimed one, pointing to page C 18 headed *London Stadtmitte.* 'Fantastic. What reconnaissance flying. It's as though London never had smoke or fog.'

31

'Or air defences, perhaps?' laughed another.

"I'll wager fifty marks the British have nothing as good themselves,' said the first.

'We'll know soon enough.'

The clarity was indeed extraordinary, not least in the view north east from 'Buckingham-Palast (Residenz)' towards Whitehall. The water of St James's Park lake showed dark in the photographs.

'There is some open space north of the Lake,' said the first officer, 'by that long road, the Mall. Otherwise too many trees, I think.'

The paratroop adviser cut in: 'It could be done, with a small group. With gliders, no. But with parachutists, easily. Where exactly are Churchill's headquarters?'

'Here in Downing Street, the large building by it is the Foreign Office.'

'But he must also have a bunker?'

'We believe it is in the cellar of the house,' said the Intelligence Colonel. 'Here,' he passed across one of the tourists' snapshots of 10 Downing Street.

'There is a garden at the back, surrounded by a high wall.'

Decisively, the paratroop adviser closed the meeting.

'I doubt if assassination is practicable. However please ask Intelligence urgently for details of the bunker.'


What the Luftwaffe staff officers did not know was the significance of a small, heavily sandbagged, Parkside entrance to a massive building barely one hundred yards from the lake though a considerable way from Downing Street. After much negotiation of passages and lifts, this door led to the War Premier's bunker. Long underground passages also connected it with Downing Street and with other Ministries. Here Churchill had his grey carpeted study, a simple bed at one end, a broad leather topped mahogany desk at the other. On it stood a carafe of water, a copy of Dod's Parliamentary Companion for 1940, a glass inkwell and three bell buttons. The bells summoned, respectively, his bodyguard Inspector Thompson, his butler and his Private Secretary. Britain's entire war effort was directed from here, from the Cabinet room and the map room, all on the same level, all beneath the same ten feet thick layer of concrete installed in the basement of the building in 1938. It had been one of the many hasty defence preparations made before Munich. The simplicity of the whole establishment would have astonished Goering, accustomed to the viceregal opulence of his Karinhall hunting lodge. Even Hitler's unpretentious woodland headquarters at Felsennest in the Eifel hills was luxurious by comparison.

At 0900 on September 22nd Churchill himself was looking at the long map of Britain that hung to the left of his desk. The coastline was marked in different colours. Red indicated beaches usable for the landing of both men and vehicles, black meant they were suitable only for troops. The whole stretch from Folkestone to Dungeness was red, though from Brighton to Bognor was black. The private Secretary hovered at the Prime Minister's elbow.

'Latest reports suggest they've taken Dymchurch, Camber and Pevensey, sir.' The Private Secretary pointed the places out.

'There's heavy fighting in Hythe and Seaford. Would you prefer to come into the map room?'

Churchill grunted, pulled on his cigar. 'No. But I will.'

He moved ponderously out into the white painted passage, steering himself past the obstructions of the huge wooden supports for the concrete ceiling. As he stepped into the main corridor through the doorway marked 'Prime Minister', a Royal Marines sentry snapped to attention. Churchill lifted a hand in acknowledgement.

'What's the weather outside?'

'Showery, sir.'

As Churchill passed on, the Marine silently blessed his luck. A moment earlier he'd glanced at the Weather Report Card in the

33

passage. The PM liked definite answers to his questions.

In the map room the duty officers were busy on their telephones. The senior duty officer, a Colonel, rose to his feet. Behind him a daily airforce state showed London at Red Alert and aircraft approaching from the coast. Eighteen squadrons had been airborne at dawn attacking the Junker 52s. Others were strafing the landing beaches. But the Premier wanted first to know about the Home Fleet. No, it could not be expected in the Channel area until midnight at the earliest. The cruiser Berwick and two destroyers had been damaged by U-boat attacks as they left Rosyth in the early hours. There was bad news too from Portsmouth. Another cruiser, HMS Manchester, and three destroyers, sailing to intercept the invasion fleet, had been ambushed by German destroyers and all sunk, albeit taking three German destroyers with them.

'What about the army?' Churchill demanded.

Reinforcements were being moved south with all speed, more divisions should reach Tunbridge Wells, Tenterden, Crowborough and Reading during the day. The Third New Zealand and First Canadian Brigades were among reinforcements being rushed to join the First London Division round Ashford in Kent.

It was a complicated, fast moving and in places very hazy picture that the duty Colonel painted. Churchill's reaction was terse.

'As I told the Chiefs of Staff in June,' he said, 'this battle will be won or lost not upon the beaches, but by the mobile brigades and the main reserve. Rapid, resolute engagements are what we need.' He turned to his Private Secretary.

'Assemble the War Cabinet at 10.00 o'clock. After that we must call on His Majesty and prepare a broadcast.

Already the BBC was transmitting a brief news bulletin saying that an invasion attempt had been made and was confined to a few beaches in Kent and Sussex. There followed a message from the Prime Minister urging all civilians to keep calm, stay at home and follow the invasion instructions previously distributed by leaflet and poster. The announcer quoted some key sentences.

Down in Hythe Sergeant Wyall's wife Doris heard the news bulletin as she was packing. He'd always wanted her to go and stay with relations away from the coastal bombing and she'd always refused. It was now nearly three hours since he'd gone. It was all very well Churchill saying: 'Stay at home and keep calm.' Churchill didn't have a house hardly a quarter of a mile from the fighting and on the wrong side of the canal. At first she hadn't realised the significance of her husband's hurried parting remark, 'I'm off to get the platoon on to the Nelson's Head bridge'. Then she'd remembered their job was to stop the Germans crossing, by blowing it up if necessary. So she crammed the last of her most precious possessions into a big suitcase, including the silver cup her husband had won at shooting, and put it and some bedding into the wheelbarrow. It was a real inspiration, using the wheelbarrow. Then she carefully locked the front door and started off towards the bridge, which was only a hundred yards away.

At much the same time Oberst Meindl decided his battalion was sufficiently well established to take on another task. He had a company on his bridge and a company blocking the main Folkestone road, Keeping one in reserve, that left him one spare.

'Work along the canal banks to the next two bridges,' he told the Hauptmann in command.

'They're close together. Seize the first and report by radio.'

Ten minutes later a hundred paratroopers, carbines in hand, were on the canal bank, half on each side, to cover each other's progress. They moved twice as fast as Mrs Wyall with her wheelbarrow. But they had seven hundred yards to go.

The sight of his wife labouring down the road, totally disregarding shells bursting behind her and the rattle of machine guns, affected Sergeant Wyall profoundly. He'd been worried stiff about her as other families had fled across the bridge earlier, but had resolutely stuck to his post.

'Doris,' he shouted, leaping to his feet, 'Doris, are you all right?'

'Careful, Sarge,' warned one of the others. Wyall took no notice, but helped his wife push the barrow across and round behind the Nelson's Head.

'I should have told you to leave, love,' he panted. 'I ran off too fast. I'm sorry.'

A burst of machine gun fire whanged into the bridge and shots splashed in the water.

'Oh Christ,' said the Sergeant, 'Stay back here Doris.'

He dashed round the corner of the pub to the box with the plunger and crouched over it, rifle in hand. The paratroops coming along the bank had their MG 34s in action, bullets were singing all over the place and knocking lumps of brick off the bridge. Wyall recognised the men as paratroops by their close fitting helmets and smocks as they raced from tree to tree along the other bank. He raised his rifle to fire at one, just as another he could not see lobbed a grenade. One of the flying splinters of metal drove through Wyall's battledress, through his chest, straight through his heart. He fell on top of the plunger, as he had planned to if he was hit. The bridge blew up with a tremendous roar, bricks from its single arch cascading into the canal, half burying two of the Home Guards in a slit trench on the bank. The paratroops only glanced at Wyall's body as they burst into the Nelson's head to set up the MG 34s in the windows facing the road. They took no notice of the sobbing woman with the wheelbarrow.


Up at Lympne Castle the old gardener, aware of the battle on Romney Marsh below, heard the news but could stay calm no longer. He decided to ask the soldiers what was happening. They were an odd lot those Newfoundlanders. One or two looked suspiciously like pictures of Eskimos he'd seen in a magazine and when he'd muttered something polite about Canada, they all vehemently insisted they were not Canadians. His wife agreed they were a rum lot, and with a Scotsman in charge, too. Their guns were not firing now either, which was funny. As he walked across from his cottage he saw why. The guns were on their wheels, with the men pushing and hauling to hook them up to towing vehicles. No-one even waved. He entered the Castle, through the square courtyard. It was deserted. Finally he climbed the circular stone stairs to the Observation Post in the tower and knocked on the door. A voice said 'come in'.

Captain Pearson-Smith and Bombardier Brown were still there. They looked unshaven and tired.

'What is it?' asked Pearson-Smith irritably.

'They've all gone, sir. The Newfoundlanders have gone.' It wasn't what he had meant to say at all.

'Only to their gun positions along the slope. That's where this telephone line leads.'

Pearson-Smith gestured at the field telephone in its metal box beside the radio set.

'No, sir, beg your pardon, sir . . .'

Suddenly Pearson-Smith's tiredness overcome his normal good manners.

'For Christ's sake man, get back home and look after your wife. We're busy.'

'What's happening though, sir? I've heard all the firing. Are they . . .?' His question tailed off, was left hanging.

'Short of a miracle,' said Pearson-Smith' more kindly, 'Lympne will be behind enemy lines by lunchtime. You're an old man. Keep inside with your wife. You should be all right. Now get back to your cottage. Leave the fighting to others.'

'I've got my shotgun,' there were tears in the old man's eyes. Pearson-Smith shook his head.

'Stay alive, we'll need you when we've thrown them back into the sea again.'

He watched the old man nod dumbly and stumble off through the heavy door. Then he turned to Brown.

'Seen anything more?' Brown had the binoculars.

'Far as I can make out, sir, they're about half way between the Grand Redoubt and Botolph's Bridge, about where that little railway goes across.'

37

Pearson-Smith took back the binoculars and confirmed Brown's observation through the powerful Zeiss lens, then studied his one inch map. Botolph's Bridge. There was a nice pub there, just where a minor canal passed under the road to West Hythe. Nice man the pubkeeper, too. Well, with luck he'd have evacuated by now. The regiment had done silent registration on Botolph's Bridge often enough. Soon the firing would be live. But first the railway.

'Battery target,' he called out sharply to Brown, 'Grid reference 124329. Troops assembling.'

As Brown passed on the fire orders over the radio, Pearson-Smith scanned as much of the beachhead as he could see through the smoke. There was no doubt about it, the krauts were firmly established the whole way from Hythe to Dymchurch. Tanks were crawling up through a breach in the Dymchurch wall, horses being harnessed up to guns. Barges were beached all along the shore. But, he noticed, it was now low tide and the bent scaffolding was preventing them getting off again. Out at sea a number of tugs were circling round like worried nursemaids. As for the aircraft . . .

His reverie was cut short by Brown's cry of 'Shot'. Thirty seconds later the first ranging round fell midway between the pub and the railway.

'Add 400,' he snapped.

Three minutes later the first salvoes fell among the storm-troopers of the Fifty-fifth Regiment. One of the shells killed the signaller and wrecked his heavy radio. Back in Dusseldorf his family would, in due course, hear of a hero's death and mourn, little comforted. Already this grey morning was creating a growing number of heroes for the Third Reich, despite the success of the landings.


Up in the castle tower the field telephone whirred. Brown answered it.

'They want you, sir.'

Pearson-Smith said formally, 'Officer speaking', and listened.

It was the Gun Position Officer of the Newfoundlanders at the other end. What the nasal voice related turned Pearson-Smith momentarily white. He asked a question.

'We're pulling out, brother, that's all I know,' said the voice. The phone clicked dead. Pearson-Smith turned to Brown.

'The old gardener was right. The Newfoundlanders have been ordered to pull out and save their guns because there's something like a German parachute battalion moving on Lympne airfield from behind.'

'So we're nicely sandwiched between them and the ones down at the railway?'

Pearson-Smith reflected: 'Our orders are to maintain observed fire on the troops moving inland until the last moment. That will be when they reach the military canal and we can't see them anyway. We shall have to hang on.'

'In that case, sir,' replied Brown, with a phlegm that surprised his superior, 'we'd better brew up at once. Never know where the next cuppa's coming from, I mean.' And he added, 'Should have known there was a catch in this observation post lark. Sitting here all dry and no marching. Bound to be a catch, wasn't there sir?'


A mile further along the ridge towards Aldington a farmer noticed the Newfoundlanders' guns trundling past on the road that runs at the top of the escarpment among the trees. It also sounded to him as though the battle on the Marsh was coming closer. He walked out through the thin line of wood to the top of the slope and spent a few minutes gazing at the tiny figures swarming across the fields.

'It'll not be long before they reach the canal,' he thought.

So he walked quickly back to his house, picked up the telephone and asked for an Ashford number, marvelling how calm the operator seemed. Her switchboard must be jammed with calls. However he got through.

'I reckon its about time,' he said, obscurely, in his soft Kentish voice. Evidently the reply was affirmative, because he went on

'The wife and kids should be round in a couple of hours then. I'll send them to Jack's first.'

He put the phone down and went through to the kitchen, where his wife was peeling potatoes.

'Look love,' he said, 'I've a job to do in the Home Guard. You'll be safer in Ashford. There's enough petrol in the car to get you there. Jack Marks at the chemist shop will look after you, until someone fixes you up with a bed.'

When at last his family had left, protesting and tearful, the farmer walked out to the woodshed, where he shifted a pile of logs and carefully lifted a long yellow oilskin bag from the hole they had concealed. Inside was a special high velocity ·22 rifle, a Hornet, with a bulky night sight and a silencer. He took it to the kitchen, checked it carefully, filled the magazine and applied the safety catch. Then he replaced it in the oilskin bag and stood it inside the broom cupboard. Next he went upstairs, hauled on his battledress and over that put on an old tweed coat and a baggy pair of corduroy trousers. Finally he returned to the kitchen and made a cup of tea. If possible he wanted to delay leaving until after dark. It all depended how soon the Germans crossed the canal.

North of Ashford, in the village of Bilting on the Canterbury road, similar clandestine preparations were in hand, though on a greater scale. Up a narrow farm track, where a belt of trees run down towards the village from the vast King's Wood above, stands a cottage called The Garth. Here, in a high ceilinged studio more reminiscent of a baronial hall than a cottage, a group of men in motley uniforms sat on boxes listening to a briefing. Their instructor was a young army captain, well known to the pre-war world as a traveller, author and journalist. His name was Peter Fleming and it was he who had recruited the farmer at Aldington into the Kent battalion of a resistance movement. The Auxiliary Units, which Fleming had created in Kent and Sussex before they were formed nationally, were seven-man teams whose job after invasion was to go to ground in special hideouts.

40

The national training centre was at Coleshill Park, a great mansion in the Berkshire countryside. The centre for Kent and Sussex was The Garth and the men listening to Fleming, all nominally members of the Home Guard, were on a weekend course in sabotage.

Fleming's own hideout, up in Kings Wood, was reached through a hinged tree stump. If you pulled hard enough on a rusty iron ring, the stump would swing back, revealing the concreted entrance to a hideout. All the hideouts were ingenious. But they gave no lease for a long life. They held food and ammunition for twenty days. The Auxiliaries would be lucky if they lived that long. Hence Fleming's words to his group of pupils were deliberately lighthearted this morning.

'As the invasion has so rudely interrupted our training for it,' he told them, 'I am dismissing you early.'

He consulted his watch. The time was 0950.

'Ridiculously early. Get back home, check your weapons, stand by and go to ground when you think fit. Remember, don't start operations until the enemy advance is well past you. It's their supply lines and rear echelon we want to sabotage. Good luck,' he concluded. 'Kill silently. And don't imagine you'll ever get off so early on a Sunday again.'

As they were dispersing the phone rang. It was Fleming's one local contact with the army command, an Intelligence Officer of the First London Division HQ at Ashford. Until a year ago he'd been a BBC producer and had met Fleming occasionally.

'Tony speaking. How's life?'

'Just preparing to move into winter quarters,' replied Fleming genially.

'Understood. But the boys in Berkshire desire to have words.'

Usually Fleming felt the ex-BBC producer had the right rather flippant attitude to war. This time he bridled.

'You know perfectly well that Thorne is my boss.' General Andrew Thorne, the 12 Corps Commander, whose military writ ran from Sheerness to Portsmouth, had commissioned Fleming to establish these 'stay behind parties'. It was only last month that they were amalgamated with the others and run from

41

Coleshill. Nonetheless Tony was adamant.

'You'll be back this afternoon. A Lysander is picking you up in a few minutes.'

Fleming gave way. The Lysander was an ungainly machine, excellent for short landings, but slow and vulnerable. Yet it could carry a few tiny bombs and for the RAF to release anything that could fly indicated the importance of the mission. A small strip of grassland near The Garth was kept free of the poles and derelict motor cars strewn over open fields to stop German aircraft landing. The Lysander pilot dropped neatly into this space and was soon en route to the field by the River Thames at Kelmscott which the Coleshill staff used as an occasional private airfield.

As the pilot flew low over the countryside, Fleming gazed out, fascinated. Long lines of vehicles queued on the roads. The railway from Ashford to Redhill, reputedly the longest straight stretch of line in Europe, carried a procession of trains, some with tanks on flatcars, all halted by bombing near Ashford. In small towns people were crowded in market squares. As they skirted south of Biggin Hill, he could see the Spitfires rising from the airfield there and the barrage balloons guarding London as they passed Croydon. The activity everywhere was intense. Even further west the country was visibly on the move, not as on a normal day, hither and thither, but all southwards, as though some gigantic summer outing was drawing the army to the coast. Looking down on it like this, Fleming appreciated exactly what those cold words, 'Logistic problems', meant. It was a planners' nightmare. Yet, he reflected, it must be even more of one for the Germans, with twenty five miles of sea between them and their re-supply. Fleming recollected that the MI 14 Intelligence notes on the French campaign said: 'The speed of advance caused considerable delay in bringing up rations. There were instances when troops had nothing but iron rations for three days. In spite of this they continued to fight and advance.' A tough lot the Germans. The notes also advised, 'The Germans do not admit that there are any "rules" in warfare and any form of trickery and cunning . . . must be expected'. Maybe that was why he was being flown to Coleshill.

The Lysander pilot hedge-hopped his way west for good reasons. Both the RAF and the Luftwaffe had thrown everything they possessed into support of the ground battle. With the cloudbase staying low, despite a freshening wind, the airspace was crowded. In the one morning the Luftwaffe had flown 1200 fighter and 800 medium bomber sorties, the former mainly against coastal defences, the latter against railways, main roads, airfields and radar stations.

The efficiency of the German ground crews was phenomenal. The turnround Adolf Galland's mechanics achieved, refuelling and re-arming his ME 109 in a matter of minutes, enabled him to fly three sorties of 'free chase over south east England' by lunchtime. When he landed after the third, and jumped down out of the plane, the stub of a cigar clenched between his teeth as usual, he looked slightly haggard. But he could tell his boys to 'chalk up another four' beneath the tally of earlier kills painted on the Messerschmitt's rounded tail fin.

He almost discounted two of them. They had been Tiger Moths, flimsy 85 mph biplane trainers that the RAF had fitted up with a few 20 lb bombs and sent against the barges as a desperate last resort. He had been roaring over Hastings when he spotted them. One burst of machine gun fire each had been enough. Then he had flown along the sea front at Eastbourne at below fifty feet, shooting up army positions, pulled up sharply at Beachy Head and found Stuka's were dive bombing the radar there. That was when he downed his first Spitfire, just after it had shot down one of the Stukas. The Briton had kept his eyes on his own kill for a few seconds too long. The second kill was similar. Again a Spitfire, again chasing Stukas, though this time over Newhaven, and this time the RAF pilot had been imprudently celebrating with a victory roll over the Stukas' target. Then a glance at the fuel gauge told Galland it was time to go home. That was the snag about the ME 109. It had superb performance, thanks to the petrol injection system, performance that at the crucial moment gave it superiority over the Spitfire, despite their similar maximum speeds. The conventional carburettor on the Spitfire's Merlin engine lacked the same immediate responsiveness to the throttle in certain flight manoeuvres, especially ones involving negative "G". When a Spitfire tried to escape pursuit with a diving half roll, the ME 109 pilot could push his stick forward, slam on full throttle, and catch it up easily without rolling himself. But there was never enough petrol. The ME 109 lacked range. If the projected additional invasion landing at Lyme Bay in Dorset was actually made, Galland failed to see how it was going to receive fighter cover, even from Cherbourg.

For the moment, though, that didn't arise. What did matter, he told his squadron back at their mess in the farmhouse at Wissant, was that Dowding, the British Fighter Command C-in-C had been forced to abandon husbanding his crews. Until today he had clearly been at great pains to keep a proportion of his squadrons well away from the Battle of Britain. Now, at last, he was throwing in everything he'd got – witness the Tiger Moths.

'It can only be good for us,' Galland told his pilots, adding tersely, 'And this, gentlemen, is a fight to the finish.'


Whether they tempted providence, or not, some pilots were lucky and others less so. One of the lucky ones was James Scott, a Spitfire pilot based at Tangmere near Chichester. Tangmere was a pleasant grass airfield in Sussex countryside that war could not spoil. Some of the pilots had girl friends in the town. The contrast between their moments of leisure in the local pubs on the warm summer evenings and their fighting sorties in the air was so acute that Scott often felt he was living two lives, not one. Even so he could never quite identify himself with 'The Few', to quote the phrase Churchill had coined for the Battle of Britain pilots in a memorable speech on August 20th.

'Never in the field of human conflict was so much owed by so many to so few.'

James Scott knew that roughly eighty per cent of the aerial victories were scored by the best twenty per cent of the pilots. He was emphatically not one of that twenty per cent and he always felt embarrassed by the doting letters from his aunt quoting 'The Few'. In fact the phrase that summed it up for Scott was coined by one of his immediate predecessors in the Oxford University Air Squadron: 'The last of the long-haired boys' was how Richard Hillary was fond of describing their generation which had been catapulted straight from undergraduate life learning to fly Tiger Moths two afternoons a week, into being full time Spitfire pilots. Scott was now just twenty. He hoped to go back to Oxford and take his degree after the war. But all that was totally overlaid by the Spitfire. As there was no two seat trainer version, your first flight consisted of climbing in, listening dazedly to the instructor's parting advice, revving up that colossal Merlin engine, then the surge forward as you opened the throttle getting the tail up quickly so that you could see where you were going, using a lot of left rudder to counter the strong swing to the right caused by the engine's torque, finally easing her off the ground as the speed built up. You never forgot that first solo in the Spit and every take off reminded Scott of it. He'd learnt to fly the aircraft all right and duly became a fully fledged pilot officer in this Auxiliary squadron at Tangmere after twelve hours and fifteen minutes Spitfire experience. By normal standards that meant he was totally inexperienced. He had nearer one hundred hours now. Just enough, as the squadron leader tried to remind the newer pilots, to make him dangerously self-confident. Not surprisingly his personal Battle of Britain score so far was 'Love – Fifteen. I've been shot down once'. Nonetheless his aunt firmly believed that he massacred Messerschmitt's daily before breakfast.

On Sealion Day, Scott did at last 'bag a Hun', though not a Messerschmitt and not before breakfast. His kill was a Junkers 87 dive bomber that was attacking the fort on the cliff above Newhaven harbour. The Stuka, as the Ju 87 was known had acquired a reputation for invincibility during the German blitzkrieg in Poland and in France, culminating in the strafing of the crowded evacuation beaches of Dunkirk at the end of May. The Stuka pilots came in high, peeling off one by one into a steep diving turn out of which they plunged earthwards, lining up physically on their target and releasing their bombs from a few hundred feet just before pulling out of the dive. But to do this the

45

Stuka had to be a relatively slow aircraft, a full 120 mph slower than the Spitfire. It was also inadequately defended by the 7.9 mm machine gun mounted in the rear cockpit.

Scott spotted the Stukas over Newhaven from a couple of miles off. The last of the six was a sitting duck. Scott caught it pulling out of its dive. The converging streams of bullets from the Spitfire's eight machine guns chewed pieces off its tail, which cartwheeled through the air alarmingly close to Scott. He watched it crash in the sea, hitting a barge in a great burst of flame, and couldn't resist a victory roll over the Fort for the double kill.

It was as he came out of the roll, heading towards Seaford, that his own score, now fifteen-all, abruptly changed again to fifteen-thirty. A line of holes appeared silently in his port wing, punctuated by a shattering thump as a bullet hit the armoured back of his seat. He jinked violently to starboard and looked round. An ME 109 with a Mickey Mouse painted on its fuselage flashed past, immediately flicking over into one of the tightest turns Scott had ever seen. 'Christ that was quick', he thought, banking hard to follow the Messerschmitt round and realising that of course he'd lost speed in the roll. The engine spluttered and stopped. Instinctively he pulled the stick back to gain height for a forced landing as he'd learnt during flying training, watching the airspeed fall off. He was too low to bale out, but he'd made a second mistake. A series of crashing explosions threw the Spitfire about.

'Oh Christ,' he thought 'Mickey Mouse again, and using his cannon.' Oil flew up all over the windscreen and he smelt smoke. This time he stuck the nose down, hauled back on the sliding canopy so that he could see out to the side and concentrated on finding a patch of open ground. He didn't see Galland again. He was too busy side slipping the Spitfire to keep the flames from the engine away from the cockpit. At three hundred feet a wide field with two sets of tall white painted rugby goal posts came in sight close ahead. He kicked harder on the rudder, losing two hundred feet fast, and straightened up just in time to belly-land a few yards short of the posts. Then he was out of the burning aircraft

46

and running. The petrol tanks blew up as he got clear, but he didn't look round or stop running for another hundred yards. Then he sank down on the grass of the rugger pitch, pulled off his parachute harness and sat panting for breath, watching his Spitfire burn.

'Bloody idiot,' he said to himself, 'That was lucky.'

Recovering, he looked around. Behind him stood a rambling Edwardian red brick house, with a small clock tower, evidently a school. The clock showed ten to eleven. It couldn't be! His take off had been at ten twenty five and that was a lifetime ago. He looked at his watch to check. But it wasn't there and to his surprise he noticed a deep cut on his left wrist, oozing blood. That must have happened opening the canopy. He was sucking the wound clean, and thinking his aunt would be upset because the watch was an eighteenth birthday present, when a boy came running up.

The boy wore grey shorts and grey shirt and a pink and blue school cap. He was about ten years old, maybe eleven. He was very agitated.

'Sir, sir,' he cried, 'Get up quick.' Then seeing the blood he asked, 'Are you all right?'

'I'm fine thanks.' In fact Scott felt sick and slightly lightheaded.

'Where are we?'

'Normansal School, Seaford,' replied the boy promptly.

'But you must get up, sir, the Germans are coming.'

Scott took that in all right. He scrambled to his feet.

'Let's get under cover then.'

Slinging his parachute over his shoulder, he doubled across to the school with the boy at his heels. The interior shocked him. Every other step of the staircase had been ripped up, the bannisters were missing. Windows were broken and replaced with cardboard. Bedding lay strewn around. Evidently the place had been requisitioned by the army. Trust the pongos to make a mess.

'They all left in a terrible hurry,' explained the boy. 'That's what woke us up.'

47

'Who's you?'

'Mr Seagrove and me. We came back yesterday to find books and things. The school was evacuated in the holidays. When we started the new term on Monday we discovered all sorts of things had been left behind. So we came from Herefordshire to fetch them.'

'Where's Mr Seagrove, then?'

'He thinks the soldiers must have borrowed his car. He's gone to find it. He told me to wait. I saw your crash and then I saw Germans on the other side of the golf course.'

'No point in waiting for them,' said Scott decisively. 'Do you know the country around here?'

'A bit,' said the boy, 'We can go up past the wood across the fields to the Cradle Valley. There's a farm. And from High and Over you can see for miles, right down to Cuckmerehaven.'

'Get me a drink of water while I write a note for Mr Seagrove,' said Scott, adding to himself, 'I hope to God our house is never requisitioned.'

They pinned the note on the front door, and left through the kitchens, walking past the wood and the pond the boys had dug themselves for sailing model boats, and so out across the fields to the steep gorse-strewn slopes of the Cradle Valley. But although they were moving away from Seaford, the noise of the distant battle seemed to increase. The sky was full of aircraft and though none attacked them, they prudently threw themselves flat when a German raced overhead. Rathfinny Farm proved to be deserted, so they tramped another mile to High and Over, by the Seaford – Alfriston road. From this vantage point, three hundred feet above sea level, all the noise was explained. A massive landing had been made on the small beach at Cuckmerehaven. Men were moving up both sides of the winding Cuckmere river, undeterred by the marshy ground. British soldiers were firing down at them from the far slope where the hills rise in great undulating ripples of downland to form the Seven Sisters range of cliffs. One bunch of Germans could be seen storming up the hill. But the bulk were up by a road bridge across the river: 'That's the Exceat Bridge,' said the boy.

'What happens further up the river?' asked Scott.

'Alfriston. It's down this road.'

'Then we'd better leg it there quick, or the Hun will be there before us.'

They had barely gone three hundred yards down the road when a tremendous roaring and grinding noise heralded the approach of a column of tanks. Seeing the pilot in his flying boots, parachute slung on his shoulder, the leading tank driver stopped. A Lieutenant riding in the turret removed his earphones and shouted down at them.

'Bad luck. Do you know where the Germans are, by any chance?'

'They've got the Exceat Bridge,' shouted the boy.

'I need transport back to Tangmere,' yelled Scott above the din.

'Sorry old man. Can't stop now. We're the counter attack. Try Alfriston.'

The tanks rolled deafeningly on their tracks leaving patterned scars on the road.

'Cruiser Tanks,' said the boy, proud of recognising them. 'They have Nuffield-Liberty engines. 340 horsepower.'

'Bloody pongos just the same,' commented Scott sourly as they walked on down the road. 'My Spitfire had a Rolls Royce engine. Over 1,000 horsepower.'

'I knew that,' said the boy.


At Fighter Command Headquarters Air Chief Marshal Sir Hugh Dowding was in the Operations room where Women's Auxiliary Air Force girls – WAAF's they were called – plotted the moves of squadrons on a vast map table. His assistant came quietly to his side.

'Bad news I'm afraid, Sir. A German glider regiment has landed on Hawkinge and paratroops are moving on Lympne. The army doubt if they can hold either. So by tonight the Luftwaffe will have an airfield. We cratered Hawkinge, but not Lympne.'

49

'They won't dare use it,' replied Dowding calmly. 'What are our losses today?'

'Up to 10 o'clock, only three Spitfires and five Hurricanes. But a lot of those fifty converted trainers have bought it, sir. Oh, yes and we've managed to put a mobile low level radar on to Beachy Head. It'll take at least twenty four hours to repair the old one.'

'Are the squadrons arriving in the south yet?'

'Yes, Sir.' The assistant consulted a list. '29 squadron and 23 squadron, they're both nightfighters, have moved into Martlesham. 65 is on the way from Turnhouse to Boscombe, 145 to Tangmere, 151 to Gravesend, 605 and 232 to Boscombe, 92 and 238 to Filton. Altogether twelve more will be down by tonight. Of course that includes bomber squadrons.'

'They're just as important,' said Dowding. 'We must pray for their success.'

The Prime Minister's call at Buckingham Palace was comparatively brief. After an aide had recounted the military situation, the King recorded a simple broadcast. It would be transmitted together with Churchill's speech to the nation at midday. Although London was now suffering heavy bombing attacks, the King categorically refused to leave the capital, even for Balmoral.

'Our place is here,' he told Churchill firmly, adding with a smile, 'I see no reason why you should be alone at the barricades in Whitehall.'

Churchill did not demur. Later he might have to give evacuation orders to his Sovereign.

Back at Storey's Gate General Sir Alan Brooke, who had recently succeeded General Sir Edmund Ironside as C-in-C Home Forces, was waiting in the map room. He and the Prime Minister had inspected many of the coastal defences together in recent weeks. He wanted to explain in person why the Germans were having such success in establishing their beachheads. Churchill arrived and listened impatiently as Brooke related how, for instance, there was only one battalion trying to hold four miles of the Pevensey Beach. It was the Fourth Battalion, Duke of Cornwall's Light Infantry. Its machine gun nests, in principle five hundred yards apart, were in practice much more widely separated. At dawn they had found themselves facing most of a Division, apparently the 26th. Altogether some nine different German divisions had been identified so far. On the British side the total coastal defences round the whole country amounted to twenty five divisions of which only seventeen were fully trained and equipped, while only three were in Kent and Sussex on the 21st. These three had been reinforced as rapidly as possible.

'We must counter attack,' insisted the Prime Minister. Brook replied that the First Tank Brigade was, at this moment, mounting a counter attack in the Newhaven Seaford area. The New Zealand Division would soon be in Folkestone.

By tonight General Andrew Thorne's 12 Corps would be strong enough to counter attack at various points. Churchill nodded vigorously as the exposition continued.

'The essential thing,' Brooke went on, "if for the RAF and Navy to stop them getting supplies across the Channel. Their tanks need diesel. They can't fill up with that at village petrol stations.'

Churchill turned to the duty Colonel.

'Where's the Home Fleet now?'

'Off Flamborough Head, Sir. Should be at Chatham by midnight.'

The Prime Minister's interrogation was interrupted by the Private Secretary.

'A telegram has arrived from the Ambassador at Stockholm, sir. It's on your desk.'

Churchill gestured to Brooke 'Come along.'

The telegram was marked Secret and Immediate. It bore the date time group 221100 and with usual protocol was addressed to the Foreign Office. It began: 'The Minister for Foreign Affairs summoned me at 9.00 am this morning and handed over

51

the following German terms for an immediate armistice intended to be followed by the early signature of a peace treaty. The Minister's good offices in negotiating it had been requested by the German Ambassador.' The terms consisted of nine numbered paragraphs. They included a German guarantee of all British possessions overseas with, in return, British recognition of all German conquests in Europe including the Channel Islands; the withdrawal of British support for exiled European Governments and Britain to enact laws against the Jews. 'If these generous terms are not accepted immediately,' the text stated, 'The Führer will exterminate Britain with total ruthlessness.'

Churchill read the telegram carefully. He put the sheet of paper down, looked at Brooke and the Private Secretary and, with considerable forcefulness, jerked the two forefingers of his right hand upward in his famous V sign.

'Seconded,' said Brooke.

# Chapter Three

*1200 September 22 to 0600 September 23*

The tidetables for Dover predicted that the sea would have edged back up the shingle for the second high tide of Sealion Day by 1402. Captain Bartels was in a fever of energy all morning to have his motley fleet, or what remained of it, ready for the return voyage by then. Whether a thirty-foot cabin cruiser, legitimately the property of a wealthy French industrialist's family from Lille, was the ideal command vehicle for the job was proving another question. The grey paint slapped on her sides as camouflage gave little protection against strafings from Spitfires or near misses from shells. At least not in daylight. Her best defence was keeping moving, and this she certainly did. Bartels stood in her cockpit with the megaphone shouting orders as his crew weaved the boat along the length of the shore.

'You'! he roared at the petty officer on a motorised barge that was idle, 'Hard astern out of the way. Clear the channel. Then out again to unload the steamers.'

In the hours after the landing the beach engineers had displayed tenacious courage lifting mines and cutting away sections of the defensive scaffolding though under heavy fire. Indeed the twisted refuse of the assault itself was a hazard. Damaged or sunken boats lay at all angles on the shingle and at all depths. Soon after S-hour submersible tanks had been carefully lowered into the water from specially fitted cargo vessels. Then, driven virtually blind in the disturbed sea and breathing through long snorkel pipes trailing behind them like the hose on a vacuum cleaner, the tanks crawled up out of the sea like science fiction monsters. Inevitably many had become stuck, or leaked, drowning their entombed crews. Their projecting guns and turrets were now obstacles to German movement, not British. Nonetheless by 1100 a number of 'safe' lanes led ashore, marked out with flags on the sand.

It took even less time for Bartels to decide that Grand Admiral Raeder's oft expressed fears about unloading across the beach were well founded. At 0950 he saw Generalmajor Loch and his 17 Division staff safely lightered ashore from their steamer. He ferried Loch himself, wanting to impress one thing on him urgently.

'Mein General,' he yelled above the din, 'you must capture Folkestone. We must have a port – cranes – a quayside. If the wind rises this beach will become impossible.' He gestured to the sky. 'Also this kind of landing demands absolute air superiority. We lack it.'

As he jumped into the shallows Loch replied, 'The 21st Regiment will be in Folkestone tonight.'

Bartels gave him a thumbs up sign and called 'hard astern' to his petty officer. He hoped the General was right. Germany was a nation of landsmen, not sailors. The army quite simply lacked comprehension of what crossing the sea entailed. They thought of the Channel as a glorified river. In Feldmarschall von Brauschitsch's orders the Kriegsmarine had been made responsible for 'the technical execution' of the landing. What a phrase! Exactly the efficient sounding form of words some army staff officer could be trusted to use, neatly glossing over the Wehrmacht's almost total ignorance of amphibious warfare. The most recent successful German amphibious operation on anything approaching this scale that Bartels could call to mind was the landing of 12,000 men in three hours on the Baltic island of Rugen. That had taken place in November 1715. Subsequently 5,000 horses had been ferried across. And here the army was, two hundred and thirty five years later, still dependent on thousands of horses, still using civilian barges. Mein Gott!

In fact Bartels had led the Kriegsmarine's experimental station at Emden earlier in the year, working over all the problems of amphibious assault. He was better qualified than most to see through the execution of this one. This was why he remained with his motorboat off Hythe until the afternoon. By lunchtime Bartels was referring to her jocularly as the 'floating colander'. Most of her once glamorous flying bridge had been shot away and if the two crew had patched one hole close to the waterline, they'd patched a dozen. But somehow the two Perkins diesels kept chugging on.

The south westerly wind had now risen to Force 4 and the waves had reached almost the maximum the Rhine barges could weather. This delayed the unloading of fourteen steamers from Rotterdam, which had brought in the 17th Division's second echelon shortly after 1100. The steamers had to anchor well out, transferring their loads to barges. At 1505, only minutes before they would have completed discharging, a determined raid by two hundred RAF light bombers sank three of the fourteen.

The raid could hardly have been worse timed for Bartels. He was in the throes of marshalling the lumbering procession of craft half a mile offshore for the voyage back, scurrying round like a sheepdog in his motorboat, when the bombers struck. The escorting minecraft were in position on the flanks. Evasive action was impossible. At least fourteen barges and three tugs were sunk and, though some of the crews were rescued, over three hundred British prisoners of war drowned, many of them Home Guards virtually within sight of their families. Bartel's orders had specially stressed the bringing back of POWs for detailed interrogation on the exact state of England's defences.

The captain of the tug *Anne Marie* was more fortunate. True, his first hopeful scheme for his own self-preservation was scuppered. It was based on finding a couple of empty barges straight after the landing, before the tide receded, and making them his passport for an early return to Dunkirk. Instead he found Bartels alongside in the cabin cruiser, shouting through a megaphone for him to wait and help lighter loads in from steamers. But then towards mid-morning a small group of shipping assembled, including General Loch's steamer, which had fouled and damaged a propeller. The *Anne Marie* was detailed to escort her back, unencumbered by any barges, in case she needed assistance. In the event all went well. So the tug, with her splintered wheelhouse and bullet-pocked sides, missed the RAF raid and made the crossing at seven knots instead of three.

When they berthed at Dunkirk which, judging from the debris on the quaysides, had been receiving the RAF's attentions during their absence, the *Anne Marie*'s captain produced a bottle of cognac from a cupboard in the little cabin below decks. He and the mate drank a toast.

'To safe delivery and a speedy return to Hamburg.' They both yawned.

'The *Anne Marie* wasn't built for wars,' said the captain, 'And this is the second she's been in.' The heavy brass manufacturer's plate in the engine room bore the date 1908. The captain sank his heavily jowled face in his hands, his elbows on the cabin table. He was suddenly intensely depressed. 'The old girl can't take much more.'

'Cheer up Fritz. We'll repair the wheelhouse tomorrow,' said the mate. 'Now what about some decent German food instead of the muck they serve in these dockside cafes?'

They cooked sauerkraut and boiled potatoes on the small stove, and ate it with good German bratwurst, washing the meal down with Pilsen beer. Afterwards, exhausted, they fell asleep on the cabin's two cloth-covered benches.

Many hours later, not long before dawn, Captain Bartels finally shepherded his motley flotilla into the harbour. Tired as he was, he noticed the fresh bomb damage. Of the barges in reserve for the second wave of the invasion, four had been sunk at their moorings. He estimated the losses in the Channel crossings at not less than fifty.

Nowhere, except among the battalions on the beaches, was it possible to start counting the cost of Sealion accurately on the 22nd. There were too many imponderables. In any case there was one overridingly immediate question both for Grand

Admiral Raeder and for Reichmarschall Goering, though for differing reasons: it was the location of the British Home Fleet. The Admiral had not forgotten the mid-April battle at Narvik in Norway when ten of his destroyers – half of all the destroyers the Kriegsmarine possessed – had been lost to Royal Navy intervention. Now the Zerstorers numbered 6, 10, 14, 15 and 16 were at Le Havre. Zerstorer 20 was in the North Sea. Three others were in Cherbourg. The Heavy cruiser *Hipper* and the pocket battleship *Scheer* were off Ireland, attempting to draw away the Home Fleet by creating a diversion. Overall, the Kriegsmarine had woefully insufficient strength to tackle the Home Fleet head on. Raeder had to place his faith in the minefields and in Admiral Doenitz' U-Boat flotilla. Sealion planning included stationing U-boats in small packs off the Scilly Isles, off the Isle of Wight, off the Humber mouth and the Pentland Firth. Given guidance, they could tackle the Home Fleet before it reached the Channel, as they already had done in their successful ambush off Rosyth. Since then they had lost the British. Nor had the *Köln*, one of the Kriegsmarine's two light cruisers, succeeded in making contact, although she had been ordered out of Kiel ahead of the Sealion launch on the 21st to reconnoitre the North Sea. She was still searching. So were the Luftwaffe's long range bombers, which made fruitless sweeps over the sullen east coast waters throughout the late morning and early afternoon.

Ironically it was on the Luftwaffe that Raeder might finally have to depend. Goering had long advocated his aircraft as the only tool of war necessary for reducing Britain to starvation; he had even gone out of his way indeed to insult the Kriegsmarine. The animosity between the two Service Chiefs was always latent, often open. Yet both Raeder and the British had come to believe that air power constituted the gravest danger to ships. On May 8th Churchill himself, explaining why the Navy did not follow up the Narvik success by attacking the German supply line to Norway across the waters of the Skagerrak, had told the House of Commons that 'losses inflicted from the air would very soon constitute a naval disaster'. The quotation had gone straight into the German Naval Operations diary, where the opinion was already expressed that 'the operation of heavy combat forces in the coastal zone . . . especially within reach of Stukas . . . would subject the naval units committed to the gravest dangers'.

The Luftwaffe argument was partially proven shortly after 1400 when the three cruisers *Galatea, Aurora* and *Penelope*, together with four Tribal class destroyers were despatched to bombard the invasion beaches at Hythe, Dymchurch and Dungeness and to attack the barges Bartels would later be bringing back. Throwing heavy ships into action in such proximity to an enemy-held coast was a desperate move. Off Dover they came under fire from the thirty heavy guns of the Gris Nez batteries that so delighted the Führer, and ran against a force of twenty E-boats on duty screening the invasion shipping lane. On top of that the Luftwaffe sent in fifty Stukas and forty ME 109s to attack them. The destroyers survived, being faster and able to turn quicker, whilst also providing less of a target. But the officer of the watch on Ashanti's bridge was horrified to see first *Penelope* and then *Galatea* vanish momentarily in great cascades of water as the Stukas' bombs fell around them, both emerging visibly out of control. A minute later a bomb – or was it perhaps a shell from Cap Gris Nez – set off one of *Penelope*'s magazines. A great rush of flames swept up from the centre of the ship. The watchers on Ashanti could see men leaping overboard to save their lives, as the ME 109 pilots sprayed the decks with machine gun fire. *Penelope* sank. Within half an hour *Aurora* had followed her to the bottom, and *Galatea* was disabled. The destroyers rescued as many survivors as they could, until the concentration of the enemy attacks forced them to disengage, and escort Galatea back to the Thames Estuary and Chatham. It was scarcely worth the destruction of six E-boats. That evening the German radio lavished praise on the Stuka pilots for their magnificient courage and success.

But these cruisers were not the Home Fleet. The only success either Raeder or Goering scored in bringing that to battle and so diverting it from its passage south, had failure as the ultimate outcome.

Alongside Sealion, the planners had devised a diversionary

expedition codenamed 'Herbstreise' or 'Autumn Journey'. This was designed to cause confusion to the British by making an apparent attack towards Hartlepool from Norway. Ten troop-ships, in fact empty, set off on this operation. They were soon spotted by a Walrus aircraft of Coastal Command. The pilot of the ungainly flying boat saw the convoy and radioed its position to the Home Fleet. The information resulted in two ships, *Norfolk* and *Naiad*, being sent to intercept this convoy. The German failure came with the convoy's dispersal and sinking later in the evening of the 22nd.

'Expensive and wasteful' was Raeder's bitter comment. The diversionary expedition had been supported by Goering!

The late afternoon brought renewed skirmishes in the Channel. The MTBs who had challenged the invasion fleet during the night were now refuelled and re-armed. They returned to harass enemy shipping in the Channel again. Minesweeping operations began off the Goodwin Sands to clear the Caeser minefield that Commodore Ruge's ships had so swiftly laid in preparation for Sealion.

From Portsmouth, HMS *Coventry* and four destroyers steamed forth yet again to attack shipping at the western end of the invasion lanes. One of the destroyers was lost to E-boats, but the action contributed to those serious casualty figures that would reach Admiral Saalwachter the following morning.

The naval battles, however, were as far over the horizon as next Wednesday's sunrise for General Loch and the other divisional commanders busy establishing themselves ashore. With two or three day's supplies assured, their attention was totally occupied by the need to strike hard and fast inland.

The initial objective of von Rundstedt's Army Group 'A', of which both the 9th and 16th Armies formed part, was a slice of Kent and Sussex south of a line following the Great Stour river from Canterbury down to Ashford, then along to Tenterden, Etchingham, Uckfield and then west of Lewes to Brighton. On the war planning maps at von Rundstedt's headquarters this objective was delineated with comfortable certainty. Thick bold arrows sped out from the divisional beachheads to the objectives. The 8th Division that landed at Newhaven along the stretch of beach leading to Seaford would drive up the line of rail to Lewes, the quiet county town above the river Ouse. From Cuckmerehaven the 6th Division, which Scott and the schoolboy had watched at the Exceat bridge, would race past Alfriston, along the Cuckmere River, then swing left towards Ringmer and Glynde through this gentle West Sussex countryside. From Pevensey and Bexhill the 26th and 34th Divisions would strike north west to Uckfield. These were all elements of the 9th army commanded by General Oberst Strauss. On the maps a neat dotted line running straight from St. Leonards through Hadlow Down and eventually on to Reigate showed the boundary between Strauss's army and General Oberst Busch's 16th army.

For Busch, still directing operations from the remoteness of his villa at Tourcoing, the first aim of seizing the bridges on the Royal Military Canal was now achieved. Where the 1st Mountain Division had established itself between Hastings and Winchelsea would provide the base for a thrust towards Heathfield. It had not escaped Busch, who was something of a military historian in his spare moments, that his mountain troops would pass close to the site of that battle of nearly nine hundred years before: Hastings.

'They'll have crossed the Channel slower than Caesar did with his hundred ships,' Busch commented sarcastically 'let us hope they move faster than King William did when they do get ashore.'

He had no doubt that they would. Nor that the 7th Division, who had already taken Rye by midday after their landing on Camber sands would push quickly on to Hawkhurst.

Only on the extreme right flank was there any uncertainty. There, the 17th Division had to force its way out both north towards Ashford and Canterbury and east up the coast towards Folkestone, Dover and Deal. Dover, with its great white stone castle standing square and formidable above the harbour, was a nut that only the toughest could crack. Even General Students's airborne staff, examining aerial photographs of the castle and town, did not suggest that the seizure of the Belgian fort of Eban Emael by landing gliders actually on it could be emulated here. Whoever fought for Dover would fight hard and long, and at great cost.

Hence the town of significance in General Busch's plan was Folkestone. It was to ensure the capture of this port and to strengthen the difficult task of the 17th Division on the right flank that the 7th Paratroop Division had been sent in at dawn to assist them. When Meindl had joked with his Adjutant about lunching with General Loch in the Imperial Hotel at Hythe his remarks had contained an underlying seriousness. He expected the fall of Hythe to follow swiftly upon the descent of his paratroops on the town and the securing of the bridges.

As it was, after the death of Sergeant Wyall and the blowing up of the Nelson's Head Bridge, the British regular troops along the Hythe seafront were completely cut off. Meindl held one bridge, his junior battalion commander held the bridge by the station, the Ladies Walk Bridge had been dismantled before the invasion. It ought to have been a recipe for surrender. Instead, the men on the seafront fought to the last round.

It was well into the afternoon before Loch's 17th Division headquarters were properly established at the Imperial Hotel, or could send a liaison officer down the few hundred yards to Meindl at the bridge. They met at 1600 hours in the hotel lounge on the first floor overlooking beaches now strewn not merely with scaffolding and barbed wire, but with corpses gently moved by the waves and the carcasses of those horses whose stampeding under fire had obstructed the landings more than it helped them. At least stretcher parties had now removed the gray uniformed bodies of dead soldiers for burial.

The cheerless sight did little to dampen the spirits of either Loch or Meindl.

'So,' said Loch, 'here we are on English soil at last. Congratulations Herr Oberst.'

'Congratulations mein General,' responded Meindl. And then, never a man to waste one of the few jokes he thought of, he added, 'I had hoped you would keep the chef here.'

'There was no need,' said Loch, 'I brought my own.' He snapped his fingers and a corporal came running.

'Coffee,' said Loch 'or would you prefer something stronger?' 'A glass of Schnapps would be very welcome,' said Meindl. When it had been brought they got down to business.

'As soon as the 21st Regiment have consolidated in Hythe,' said Loch, 'I shall set them moving along the coast road to Sandgate and Folkestone. Can any of your battalions attempt the encirclement of Folkestone from the east?' He spread out a map on the table and together they pored over it.

'Stentzler and Brauer should have command of the heights above Folkestone by now,' said Meindl. 'Their aim is to take Paddlesworth, Etchinghill and Lyminge by the end of the afternoon. Of course the Divisional Commander is with the 3rd Regiment attacking Lympne airfield at the moment. I've had no communication with him since we dropped.'

'But the two battalions you have here are at my disposal, are they not?' interjected Loch.

'That is correct, General,' acknowledged Meindl. 'There is also a glider-borne battalion due to land on the RAF airfield at Hawkinge. They should join up with Brauer and Stentzler to make a thrust down to the east of Folkestone.'

'In that case,' said Loch decisively, 'your two battalions can join with the 21st Regiment in the drive on Sandgate tonight.'

The two officers bent over the map again, tracing possible lines of attack with a pencil and with finger tips. They were interrupted by Loch's ADC, a Captain, who saluted and said:

'Two urgent signals from 16th Army, General.' He stepped smartly forward and handed the two pieces of hand-written paper that the Divisional Signals Office had copied out. 'The first, strictly speaking, is for our information only, sir,' he said. 'It originates from Luftflotte 2.'

Loch took and read them. He turned to Meindl, 'Bad news,' he said, 'and also good news. Your divisional commander was killed in the parachute drop. Feldmarschall Kesselring has appointed you Acting Major General to command the 7th

62

paratroop division. My congratulations,' he added, and gave Meindl the signal form. The second signalled message evidently perplexed Loch more. At length he turned to Meindl and said: 'This is an order from the Führer. All members of the English Home Guard shall be treated as saboteurs and shot. As I understand it, they are fighting in uniform are they not?'

Meindl nodded. 'They were the guards on the bridge down there. They are in uniform.'

Loch looked straight at Meindl. 'That is an order which I feel we should acknowledge promptly and forget as promptly. For the honour of both our Services.'

'Quite apart from its legality under the Hague Convention,' commented Meindl, 'It would expose our own men to being shot on capture.'

The two sat in thought for a moment while the ADC stood stiffly to attention at one side. Meindl looked up again, 'But there is one thing, General Loch,' he said, 'I am as concerned for my own troops' safety and well-being as anyone. If there is sabotage against them, we shall have to deal ruthlessly with it.

'Agreed,' said Loch. He turned to the ADC 'Acknowledge the second signal. And inform Luftflotte 2 that Oberst Meindl has received their signal.'

Meindl cut in, 'Add that I shall establish my headquarters on Lympne airfield as soon as possible.'

The ADC saluted and went out. Meindl smiled one of his rare smiles at Loch: 'Now, I suppose I have to climb up that damned hill again,' he said, 'and in the rain.'

'I think we can find transport for a fellow Major-General,' said Loch.


As the afternoon wore on and the rain fell more heavily Lieutenant Pearson-Smith and Bombardier Brown realised that they would have to abandon their post in Lympne Castle. Down below them at the foot of the steep escarpment the bridge across the Canal at west Hythe had been blown before the men of the 55th Regiment could reach it. So had the little bridge that carried the farm track across below Port Lympne, the country house a mile and a half away to the west. This meant that there was no way over the canal for the 55th between the bridge below Aldington, and the bridges in Hythe itself. So they were held along the line at the canal, their engineers hastily trying to construct pontoons to get across what superficially was hardly an obstacle. The canal was a mere twenty five to thirty feet wide. But its steep banks meant that bridging it was not so easy, and in any case the advance detachments and the first wave carried no bridging equipment. Meanwhile, Pearson-Smith, though denied observation of the 55th any longer, had no lack of targets elsewhere in the marsh below. The tank detachment that had made its way through the breach in the Dymchurch wall had already reached the line of the canal further west passing through Burmarsh and Eastbridge. Pearson-Smith and Brown had been continually occupied passing targets to the guns and peering through the binoculars to see what they had or had not hit amid the smoke of the battle below.

Behind them, the battle for Lympne airfield was nearly over. Stukas screaming down to divebomb the hangars and huts of the RAF station there had come over in waves at lunchtime. Miraculously, the Castle had remained untouched. In fact, Pearson-Smith's main source of information had been periodic visits from the gardener who had now assumed the unofficial position of sentry to the pair of Observers. At about 1500 he had come once again thumping up the tower steps and knocked on the door with the German uniformed devil painted on it.

'You can't stay here much longer, sir.' He shook his head, emphasising the point.

'There seem to be a few of our boys holding out by one of the hangars. But it's nearly over now. You'd better go while you can, sir.'

'Well,' said Pearson-Smith 'all good things come to an end don't they, Brown?' He picked up the radio headset and spoke briefly to his Regimental headquarters back at Aldington.

'Returning to your location, soonest.'

'We hope,' said Brown.

They packed up the spirit lamp and the old kettle carefully into a haversack, and Brown struggled to fit the harness of the radio over his shoulders. One of the snags about being a Bombardier was that you carried the radio. Pearson-Smith had his map out on the ledge, and tried asking the gardener for directions.

'Which route do you think we ought to take,' he said.

'Can't never follow these maps I'm afraid, sir,' said the gardener. 'What you ought to do is go along close under the escarpment through the woods, and if you follow along the hill you will come out near Aldington. I wouldn't follow the road if I were you, sir, not with this fighting going on.'

So they followed him down the stairs for the last time and he showed them the way out onto the Castle terrace and down the end of it where the path led along to the wood. There he waved goodbye and wished them good luck.

'You go back and look after your wife as I said,' Pearson-Smith told him, 'you've done enough for one day.'

It was rough going along the side of the hill through tussocky grass on a steep slope. Twice, German soldiers down on the far side of the canal fired shots at them, although at six or seven hundred yards they were unlikely to score a hit. The distance as the crow flies from Lympne to Aldington is only three miles and the location of the Regiment back near the woods north of Aldington put, perhaps, a further mile on the journey. Pearson-Smith thought at first he might do the whole march in just over an hour. In fact, the configuration of the hill and the woods, made his progress extremely slow. It was 1600 before he reckoned they were near a spot marked on his maps as 'The Honeypot', just below the Upper Park Farm. He and Brown paused for a drink from their water bottles and sat on the edge of the hill looking down. A mile, or maybe a mile and a half, below and to the right of them was one of the bridges of the Canal. To Pearson-Smith's horror he realised that the Germans had captured the bridge intact. A line of tanks were already moving across it.

'Quick, get the set opened up and call the Regiment,' he called to Brown.

Then he looked round quickly for a decent hiding place. Once shells started to fall on the bridge below, the men would start searching for their cause. He wriggled down behind some small bushes motioning Brown to join him. Brown was having difficulty with the aerial. Finally he got it extended and started calling, repeating his call-sign and the Regiment's, over and over again. At last, an answer came through. It was faint.

'Moving to new location,' it said. There followed an encoded grid reference. Then it went on: 'Cannot accept further fire orders for 15 minutes – over.'

Pearson-Smith pulled the griddle card for decoding the grid reference out of his pocket, adjusted the cursors, and puzzled out the meaning.

'Oh God,' he said. 'They're moving back another three miles to Mersham.'

The radio crackled again with more messages. German paratroops were now moving on Sellindge. Pearson-Smith consulted the map 'What it amounts to,' he explained gloomily to Brown, 'is that the tanks are coming up from the south and the paratroops are coming in from the north, and we're the ham in the sandwich.'

'Should have used the vehicle,' remarked Brown.

'No, the gardener was probably right,' said Pearson-Smith, 'we'd have only got shot up going on the road past the airfield, and there's no other way round.' Pearson-Smith looked at the map again.

'Our best hope is to keep off the road,' he said, 'and go cross-country to Aldington, then across again, and with luck we'll stay ahead of this German pincer movement.' They struggled up the few yards to the road, looked cautiously both ways and crossed by Upper Park Farm, then set out roughly north-westerly for Aldington.

By this time it was already late afternoon. The sun would set at one minute to six. They could reckon on half-an-hour of twilight after that. Then they would be moving completely in the dark, and the twilight might not last so long. The sky was very overcast and it was now raining heavily. They were gradually becoming soaked through. Their boots squelched. About four hundred yards past the farm Pearson-Smith thought he heard a soft whistle. He stopped. The whistle sounded again. He looked behind. Was that a man in the field waving? It was. Cautiously the man began to approach them. He seemed to be carrying something and as he got closer, Pearson-Smith noticed that it was a long lumpy oilskin bag. When they met, the man motioned them to walk over by the hedge.

'Can I help?' he asked.

'We're trying to make our way past Aldington and on to Mersham,' explained Pearson-Smith. 'My Regiment's just moved and we're trying to catch up with them.'

'This countryside will be alive with Germans tonight,' remarked the farmer uncompromisingly.

'That was rather my feeling,' agreed Pearson-Smith.

'What's your job exactly?' asked the farmer.

Pearson-Smith checked a desire to tell him to go to hell for curiosity and replied:

'I'm a Forward Observation Officer. I direct the gun fire, and this is my signaller, Bombardier Brown.' The farmer stood for a moment eyeing them quizzically, then he apparently came to a decision.

'If you don't mind roughing it,' he said, 'you could come along with me for the night.' He hesitated. 'At least we'll know where things stand in the morning, and who knows, we might find one or two targets for those guns of yours.'

Something about the man's air and appearance made Pearson-Smith inclined to trust him, though there was a mysteriousness about the proposal with which he felt ill at ease.

'Nothing ventured, nothing gained, sir,' chipped in Bombardier Brown.

'There's two things,' said the farmer. 'First, I'll not be moving until it's dark, and second, I'll be asking you to keep your mouths shut afterwards.' He started off towards the farmhouse.

'I forgot to tell you my name, it's Pearson-Smith,' said the Lieutenant. 'What's yours?'

'That's another piece of information you'll have to be managing without,' said the farmer brusquely. 'Sorry, but you'll understand why later.'

He led them into the farm house and bustled off to make some tea in the kitchen.

'Have you eaten lately?' he called out.

The two admitted that they had not. By the time they had consumed a quantity of bread and cheese, washed down with hot strong tea, it was dark. Without a word the farmer led them out and along the hedgerows until, after some twenty minutes, they reached a small wood. There he seemed to rummage around in the bank of a ditch until suddenly he pulled on something and a piece of the bank swung away.

'After you,' he said.

They found themselves in an underground chamber about twelve feet by eight feet, low ceilinged, and apparently made of railway sleepers and corrugated iron. It had an earth floor, tramped down to make it firm, and overlaid with duck boards. There were rought wooden bunks in tiers, and on shelves stood tins and jars and other supplies. The supplies included a surprising number of boxes of ammunition and of what, as far as Pearson-Smith could see were sticks of gelignite in bundles. The farmer took off his coat and trousers revealing his Home Guard uniform.

'For crying out loud, what is this?' asked Bombardier Brown.

'Kind of special unit,' said the farmer shortly. 'The others will turn up soon, I expect.'

Sure enough, about half-an-hour later two more men let themselves in through the concealed entrance in the bank. They eyed Pearson-Smith and the Bombardier with mistrust.

'Who are they?' they asked the farmer.

A whispered confabulation in one corner between the three of them followed, much to the embarrassment of Pearson-Smith and Brown. Finally, one of the new arrivals who was evidently the commander of this strange unit turned to Pearson-Smith.

'He should never have asked you down here,' he said. 'There are two things you can do. We stay here until the enemy have passed right over. You could help us if you could make that radio work. Or you could leave in the morning and we'll try and brief you on a few good targets before you go. Or of course, you could go now, though I wouldn't advise it if you don't know the countryside.'

Pearson-Smith thought of the pouring rain outside, the dark, and the fact that he was never much of a cross country marcher at the best of times.

'Let's see what the morning brings,' he said.


Captain Peter Fleming did not return to Bilting in the afternoon, for all the Intelligence officer's promises. Darkness fell and no Lysander had landed in the field near The Garth. Instead one flew in much later, not much short of midnight. Luckily the cloud was thick and shut out such light as a moon entering its last quarter could have given. The aircraft's door had been taken off and the slipstream howled around the cabin. The pilot, flying almost in the cloud, picked up the faint reflection of the military canal and when he judged he was a mile past Aldington, turned and shouted to Fleming:

'Saved you a few miles walk. Best of luck.'

Fleming felt for the wing strut and tumbled out. It felt all wrong parachuting into one's own countryside, unbelievable that it was now behind enemy lines. However his mission demanded the men in the hideout near Aldington, which he knew because he'd approved its siting, and Colonel Gubbins was probably right that it would be easier to jump in than to walk. Much easier.


James Scott had also found something easier than walking. At Alfriston a ration truck was setting out for Lewes. He and the boy squashed into the cab's one passenger seat.

'Not supposed to give lifts, you know sir,' the driver protested. 'Not in a ration truck.'

69

'If you don't want any bloody air support, don't take us,' Scott replied brusquely.

'No offence meant, sir,' said the driver and hastily started up.

From Lewes Scott telephoned the Tangmere Station Adjutant. 'OK, we'll send transport,' he said wearily. 'Glad you're safe.'

'The White Horse in the High Street will find me,' replied Scott cheerfully.

The main problem was the boy. In the end he went to Tangmere too. When the Squadron Leader heard the whole story he remarked 'The boy deserves a medal. He'd better stay as a mess guest until we can get him back to Hereford. As for you, James, one more wizard show like that and you'll be duty officer for life. Tomorrow morning go and sort yourself out another Spit'.

In London foreign newspaper correspondents were getting wind of the German progress, despite the censorship. Heavy raids on the capital lent some credence to Dr. Goebbels' claims on the German radio, which mentioned the bombing as an adjunct to the invasion of the south coast where British troops had put up only 'weak and sporadic resistance'. The BBC gave restrained bulletins about incursions in various areas, which all three Services were combating successfully. There were repeats of Churchill's midday broadcast, stating the British people's resolve to contest every foot of land whatever the cost in life and property.

Telegrams from the State Department asked the American Ambassador to report urgently on the situation and advised that an appeal had been made by Hitler to the President for the United States to observe 'strict neutrality' in the conflict. Perhaps as a result of Ambassador Kennedy's pessimistic estimates of Britain's ability to survive, officials in Washington half expected a collapse like that of France.

From his advance Headquarters in Whitehall, General Sir

Alan Brooke spoke on one of the black and green scrambler telephones to General Thorne, whose 12 Corps had been receiving reinforcements throughout the day. Soon there would be 130,000 men in the south east, as against 75,000 three days ago.

'How are things shaping?' asked Brooke.

'The Hun has consolidated a considerable bridgehead. It's pretty well continuous from Hythe to Rye. They're by-passing the big towns. Eastbourne hasn't been touched nor Hastings. But they're pressing hard into Folkestone from Sandgate and they've already gained a foothold on the west wide of the Newhaven harbour. It's ports they're after.'

'What happened to the Armoured Brigade at Seaford?' Brooke queried.

'Drove through so hard it reached the seafront, then had to withdraw a bit in case it was outflanked. I'm sending the Australians in to help 45 Div and the machine gun brigade at Newhaven.'

General Thorne hesitated. What he was going to propose would sound like reverting to a discredited policy.

'I know the feeling there is against defensive lines. Even so we are strong enough to form a kind of outer ring around the German bridgeheads, without prejudicing our counter-attacks.'

'What had you in mind?' asked Brooke, straining to hear. The snag about the scrambler was that its workings often produced a lot of background noise.

'Roughly south of Ashford, Etchingham, along the ridge to Heathfield . . .'

'That's a bloody long line,' said Brooke. 'The PM's bound to object.'

'Only seventy miles or so,' countered Thorne. 'No comparison with Ironside's GHQ line.' The GHQ line had been an anti-tank ditch hundreds of miles in length that supposedly protected London and the industrial Midlands. It had been officially discarded when Brooke succeeded Ironside in July. At the other end of the telephone Brooke grunted audibly.

'It could help stabilise the situation,' urged Thorne.

'Call it the Winston Line,' agreed Brooke gruffly, 'if you must name it.'

General Thorne turned to his Military Assistant, a major. 'Fetch the G staff and we'll decide who to shift.'

That was how the 2nd Canadian Brigade found themselves abruptly ordered out of the attractive village of Withyham. The Division of which they were part was the only fully equipped one in Southern England in June after Dunkirk, they had been here since July 2nd, they 'had their feet under the table' in the old soldiers' phrase. Camped in a country house park, the men paid frequent visits to the village, with its traditional Sussex weatherboarded houses. 'Clapboard' they insisted on calling it in friendly altercations with the locals in the Dorset Arms where Sergeant Major Mackenzie of the Brigade Headquarters used to tease the villagers gently about the Dorset Arms being in Sussex and the beer being called bitter when it wasn't. They took the ribbing in good part, so when the movement order came he found a few minutes to slip up to the sixteenth century oak beamed bar and say goodbye.

'Some place called Heathfield we're going to,' he explained. 'Say, we'll miss you, all of us. But I'm sure as hell glad we never had to man that pillbox by the lake. Faces nowhere and sticks out like a sore thumb.'

'I heard it was part of something called the GHQ line,' said the landlord.

'I'd sell it to some guy as a sepulchre, if I were you,' said the Canadian. 'And I should know – we're the GHQ Reserve. So long.'

'All the best,' called the landlord. 'Give Jerry one for me.'

An hour later the advance party was in Heathfield.

'Mr. Mackenzie,' said the Brigade Major, 'you're a man with an eye for the good things in life. Go find the Brigadier a billet. The goddam British seem to have taken every house worth having.'

It was true. The straggling town was crammed with equally straggling bits and pieces of a dozen units, from military police to artillery. Nonetheless Sergeant Major Mackenzie nosed out a secluded part called Old Heathfield, with a quaint pub named the Star. Pretty soon he found a small sign at the end of the a gravelled drive which read 'The Glen'.

'That'll suit my Scots ancestors,' he thought and drove down between the rhododendron bushes. The lady who answered the door of the big rambling house was raven haired, tall, elegant and an obvious foreigner.

'But of course your Brigadier must be looked after,' she smiled. 'Please come in.'

Mr. Mackenzie wiped his boots and followed her. She made him coffee and said she was Belgian.

'My husband is in the RAF. He is away of course.'

'In luck again,' thought Mr. Mackenzie. Then she enquired about the numbers involved.

'Sixty!' For a moment her composure trembled. 'If some of you sleep in the stables, I'm sure we can manage. I suppose only the officers will use the house?'

'Yes ma'am,' acknowledged Mr. Mackenzie, flattened. He thanked her, saluted, and left.

'Hell,' he consoled himself. 'You can't win 'em all.'

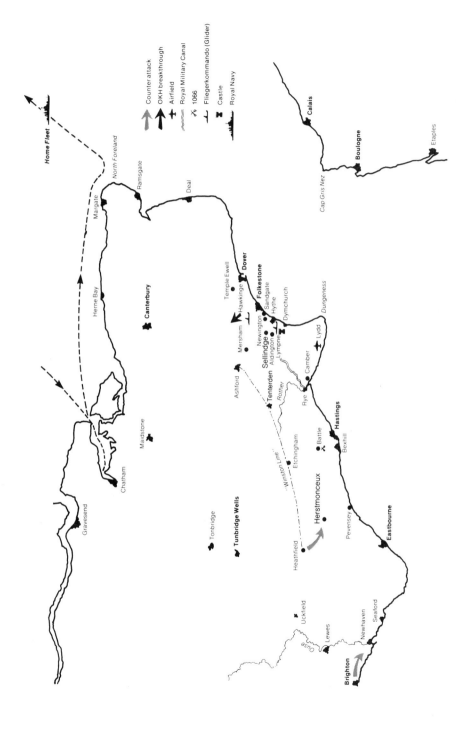

Home Fleet

Counter attack
OKH breakthrough
Airfield
Royal Military Canal
1066
Fliegerkommando (Glider)
Castle
Royal Navy

Calais
Boulogne
Etaples
Cap Gris Nez

North Foreland
Ramsgate
Margate
Deal
Herne Bay
Canterbury
Temple Ewell
Dover
Hawkinge
Folkestone
Mersham
Newington
Sandgate
Sellindge
Hythe
Aldington
Dymchurch
Lympne
Ashford
Tenterden
Rother
Camber
Lydd
Dungeness
Rye
Maidstone
Chatham
Gravesend
Hastings
Battle
Bexhill
Etchingham
Winston Line
Herstmonceux
Tonbridge
Tunbridge Wells
Heathfield
Pevensey
Eastbourne
Uckfield
Lewes
Ouse
Newhaven
Seaford
Brighton

# Chapter Four

*Dawn to 1400 hours September 23rd*

For both sides the morning of September 23rd was the moment of initial reckoning. On the ground battalion and divisional commanders took stock of their tactical positions at dawn, quartermasters checked ammunition stocks, Adjutants and Sergeant Majors went through the sad task of compiling casualty lists. Even in the heat of the worst battles the instructions contained in that fat little volume 'Staff duties in the Field', had to be observed. And with good reason. The job of collating intelligence is an enormous one. If it did not start early there was no chance that the commanders could make the decisions they needed for the day's operations.

In London, in the map room at Storey's Gate the RAF State Board showed 167 fighters of the RAF lost or damaged, with 90 pilots killed, 57 light bombers gone and with them 30 pilots, 13 medium bombers with all the pilots dead. In sum 237 aircraft out of action from a total strength of 1048 operational aircraft, plus another 192 in store. Nonetheless, at his headquarters, Dowding had already ordered those squadrons retained north of Catterick for the protection of Scotland and the north to be depleted to nine fighters per squadron instead of twelve. Ferry pilots of the Air Transport Auxiliary were even now bringing the aircraft down to join squadrons in the south. Dowding's message to his crews, like his message to the Prime Minister, urged them to have faith. The RAF estimates of Luftwaffe losses were at least 400 aircraft. Intelligence officers considered the Germans could not sustain a rate of loss so high for long.

At sea, the picture was still confused. Throwing in what the Navy had available so early in the battle had resulted in losses that might otherwise easily have been avoided, particularly by air attack on the cruisers. In consequence the battleships of the

Home Fleet had been withheld from employment after their rush south. *Rodney* and *Hood* were being kept in Milford Haven, having ploughed down the west coast with the aircraft carrier *Furious,* while *Repulse* and *Nelson* had been despatched back into the open sea after reaching the North Foreland at 1730 the previous evening. There were now enough destroyers available in the Channel to engage the invasion fleet successfully when next it crossed. Nonetheless Admiral Sir Dudley Pound could not forbear remarking to his Flag Lieutenant:

'If only we could be flies on the wall in Raeder's operations room.'

They little guessed the Grand Admiral's misgivings over Sealion.

What worried both the Navy and the RAF was an apparent build up of German forces in Cherbourg. The Navy had, during the night, taken more precautions against the re-supply of the invasion forces from the ports previously used. Fast minelayers working under cover of darkness in the early hours had been active laying mines near the harbour entrance areas of Calais, Boulogne and Dunkirk. But first-light reconnaissance by the Fleet Air Arm and by a Sunderland flying boat of Coastal Command confirmed a heavy build-up around Cherbourg. Not only had a minimum of three German destroyers been seen in the harbour, but considerable build-up of railway traffic and of barges was evident in the harbour area. Photographs hastily developed and processed showed troops in large numbers on the quaysides. The only conclusion to be drawn was that a further invasion strike was to be made west of the existing beachheads.

Reluctantly, General Sir Alan Brooke ordered the 4th Infantry Division down to Chichester; the 3rd Division from Bristol to Yeovil and the 21st Tank Brigade also to Yeovil. The 11th Corps headquarters would take control of the whole area from Southampton to Brighton, relieving General Andrew Thorne's 12 Corps of a part of its responsibilities where, as yet, there was no fighting.

This necessity was a bitter blow to Brooke, when only the previous evening he had authorised the establishment of the

Winston Line and believed that by mid-day on the 23rd the German bridge-heads would be sufficiently strongly contained for further counter-attacks to be made. Nor was his temper improved when a panic report of German paratroop landings in Lyme Bay, from the Home Guard, was proved to be erroneous. For a full hour it had jammed communications with the West Country.

Thus when the Cabinet Defence Committee assembled at 1000 the atmosphere at Storey's Gate was not cheerful, though far from desperate. And even if it had been, someone would have pointed quietly to the statements of Queen Victoria which Churchill had caused to be printed and framed in various rooms: 'Please understand there is no depression in this house, we are not interested in the possibilities of defeat. They do not exist. Signed: Victoria R.I. April 1900.' The Boer War, then seeming a national disaster, had been resolved; so would this conflict.


At 10.00 o'clock there came one piece of cheerful news. The American Chargé d'Affaires, acting in place of Ambassador Joseph Kennedy, who was back in Washington for consultations, called at the Foreign Office. On the way there, driving past blitzed houses and shops still smouldering from last night's fire bomb raids, he reflected on how wrongly his Ambassador's reports had interpreted Britain's will to resist. Kennedy had prophesied collapse. Instead, the worse things became, the more the country rallied. When he was ushered into the Permanent Under Secretary's dustily palatial office overlooking St James Park, he announced in the most cordial terms that the President had rejected an appeal from the Third Reich for the United States to maintain a 'more strict observance of neutrality'. Explaining the rejection, the Chargé said with undiplomatic frankness:

'They asked us to recall that our independence was won by fighting against your British and that German soldiers were alongside ours in that fight. Apparently Mr Roosevelt told them it wouldn't wash. I'm delighted, Sir Alexander, delighted. I guess if anything our shipments to Britain will be speeded up.'

On the German side of the Channel, at least in naval circles, shipping was the key topic. Captain Bartels' experiences at Dunkirk had been mirrored elsewhere. Other invasion flotillas had suffered fewer losses than Bartels' en route across, yet all had taken heavy punishment on the beaches. Bomber raids had sunk barges in the other ports: six at Cherbourg, two at Boulogne, five at Calais. Not large numbers individually, yet they all added up. When the Commander Naval Group West, Admiral Saalwachter, held his morning conference at Wildungen, he learnt that the hastily computed total of losses for the first day included 449 barges and 28 steamers, roughly a quarter of the whole Sealion fleet. No-one knew exactly how many of the 1200 or so motorboats and other small craft were missing.

Gathering this armada together had dislocated German domestic industry. The Navy knew it would. On July 31st Grand Admiral Raeder had warned Hitler of the inevitable effects on war production if barge cargoes ceased to reach the factory cities of the Fatherland through that amazing network of canals and rivers which fuels German industry. The Führer had replied with a special order authorising the requisitions. So virtually everything that would float, from every German lake and river, from the Spirdingsee to Memel in East Prussia, was ordered to the Channel. Any man who was a Binnenschiffer – an inland waterman – was called up too.

Now, in a mere thirty six hours, a quarter of the Sealion fleet had been lost. Saalwachter demanded more protection from the Luftwaffe. He also requested a full report from Vize Admiral Lutjens and the other Sealion Fleet Commanders. In turn Lutjens ordered explanations from the Naval Station Commanders who accompanied the invasion. The signal would be the first matter Captain Bartels had to deal with when his steward woke him for breakfast.


For every other German commander, however, the mood was ebullient, indeed euphoric. The Führer, sitting in the autumn sunshine on the terrace at Felsennest, welcomed every new detail of success, brushing aside naval misgivings and such casualty figures as his aides had available. He had deliberately stayed at his country retreat in order to remain calm. There, among the Rhineland hills and away from the telephones and bustle of Berlin he could think. Churchill's outright and contemptuously worded rejection of his peace offer had both offended and mystified him. But it had also strengthened his determination. Now the good news meant that the inspiration of Sealion had been right. Today he would make his delayed transfer to the special Sealion Headquarters found for him by Jodl at Ziegenberg. The moment had come for the Supreme Commander to take personal hour by hour control. But that was no reason to be lenient to the British. He had threatened ruthlessness, and ruthlessness they would have. At 10.30 he signed a special order of the day appointing the SS leader, Reinhardt Heydrich, as Reichsprotector of occupied territory in Great Britain.

'He is to take up his appointment as soon as operational conditions permit.'

It was to be announced on the German radio immediately. In a personal message summoning Reinhardt Heydrich to Felsennest at once, the Führer indicated that in his opinion operational conditions would permit the move within twenty four hours.

For Heydrich, a tall cruelly handsome man still in his thirties, it was momentous news. Like Dr Six, the bespectacled university lecturer, who was now designated as Britain's security police chief in the rank of Standartenfuhrer, Heydrich had risen to power as a result of fanatical devotion to the National Socialist Party. As an SS Obergruppenfuhrer he would be as ruthless as his leader required. So it was something of a surprise when, having reached the headquarters in a bare three hours, his official Mercedes racing through the Rhineland villages, klaxon blaring, Reinhardt Heydrich found the Führer's mood altered. He was treated to a dissertation over lunch on the merits of the British Empire as a stabilising force in world politics. Standing over the map tables afterwards, the Führer revealed his certainty that the campaign would be over in three weeks. It would be unnecessary to occupy further than a line running east-west from the

Severn river above the port of Bristol, north of London to Maldon in Essex. The rest of England and the whole of Wales and Scotland could be confidently expected to form an equivalent to France's Vichy Government.

Heydrich accepted the news that he was to be ruler of something very much less than the whole United Kingdom stoically. He thanked his Führer profusely, and 'Sieg Heiled' with the nearest to a ramrod straight salute that any man could achieve.


For General Oberst Busch, too, the move to England was imminent. Late on the Sunday afternoon when the morse messages reaching headquarters indicated success for the initial assault and the establishment of all the 16th Army beachheads as planned, Busch had returned to his proper army headquarters at Tourcoing, near Lille. There he issued orders for the embarkation of a skeleton headquarters with the second wave of the invasion, expected to sail on the evening of the 23rd at the latest. He would himself cross with them and assume personal command of a bridgehead that by all indications would then extend the whole way from Hastings to Folkestone and up to ten English miles inland.

'Sixteen kilometres is not enough,' he told his staff. 'I shall expect a break-out by Meindl's Division today. Assuming the Luftwaffe fly in the 22nd Airlanding Division as well, there should be no stopping them.'


At the Luftwaffe's Sealion headquarters, nominated for it by Jodl, close to Hitler's at Ziegenberg, the optimism was tempered by knowledge of the casualties. They had been forced to tell the Reichsmarschall that of his beloved fighters, 165 had been lost. And of the medium bombers, the Junkers 88s, Dornier 17s and the Heinkel IIIs, no less than 134 had been shot down or so seriously damaged that they could not fly the next day. Of the Stukas, those hitherto invincible weapons of the Blitzkrieg, 34 had gone.

The figures represented a horrifying proportion of the 732 operational fighters, 622 medium bombers and 102 dive bombers which the Luftwaffe had available for Sealion. The loss vastly exceeded that of the previous worst day when, on September 15th, over 300 bombers had been despatched to London in poor weather and 49 had failed to return. The Reichsmarschall's response had been to order mass attacks in the best weather and small, heavily escorted, attacks in bad conditions. Yesterday the enormous demands of Sealion had forced an unprecedented commitment despite low cloud. Goering's Chief of Staff, General Hans Jeschonnek, stuck to his belief that thus forcing the RAF into an equally massive response was welcome, since it would enable more Spitfires and Hurricanes to be shot down. Goering had particularly ordered Hurricanes to be pursued because their 20 mm cannon were formidable weapons. Well, at least he should be pleased with the estimates of RAF losses in the past twenty four hours.

'Not less than 450 RAF aircraft destroyed,' Jeschonnek told Schwester Christa, who this breakfast time was once again taking Goering's messages for him and barking out his demands for information.

'RAF strength was 1,100 aircraft maximum before the invasion. That means we have destroyed over forty per cent.'

In reply to a further question he assured her: 'The 22nd Airlanding Division was flown to Lympne and Hawkinge as planned at 0600.'

It was always irritating to the Reichsmarschall that the 22nd, having converted from ordinary infantry last winter, had remained an army formation, unlike the 7th Fliegerdivision, which was Goering's personal creation and whose paratroops came under Luftwaffe command.

'Nein, we have no casualty reports so far, Schwester.'

She rang off and Jeschonnek replaced his telephone receiver with relief. It was humiliating enough for a General to have to answer to the Reichsmarschall's mistress, but for the 'Sister' to be that woman!

'So ein verdammtes weibsbild!', he muttered angrily.

For the second time in two days Lympne Castle had been the silent witness to an air invasion of England, the revolution in warfare that Germany had pioneered. Today no parachutes had blossomed from beneath the Junkers 52s, there were none of those audible cracks as the chutes snapped open. Instead the aircraft were towing gliders behind them, staggering along nose high under their loads. Part of the Airlanding Division's shock troops descended in DFS 230 gliders, wooden affairs that could touch down in any small open space. Their advantage over parachuting was that the nine men inside, sitting straddled over a wooden bench, could throw up the canopy and storm out, weapons loaded and cocked, as soon as the glider skidded to a stop. Better still, the man with the MG34 machine gun mounted it inside the glider and gave immediate covering fire. That was how they had taken the airfields in Holland back in May. But there were only 150 DFS 230s available. So these were cast off from the Junkers over Hawkinge, which was conveniently close to Folkestone, but still in no state to take conventional aircraft landing on wheels, while other 52s would take a chance and land the rest of the Division in the normal way at Lympne.

So the pilots flew in over Lympne, now German-held territory, and turned right towards Hawkinge, noticing the obviously heavy fighting going on in Sandgate and the western outskirts of Folkestone. The smoke of the battle obscured much of the coastline. Not all the gliders, diving steeply down, managed to land exactly on the small grass airfield. Some overshot and crashed into buildings, one even landed on the tennis court by the officers' mess. From above, the Junkers 52 pilots could see gliders strewn like toys all over the place. Some had tipped up nose first into holes that had not been properly filled. Others had torn their wings off on the hedges and trees at the side of the airfield. But already the troops were out and doubling to their forming up points as the Junkers disappeared towards Lympne, now guarded heavily by a battalion of the 3rd Paratroop Regiment who had dropped into Sellindge the day before.

With the danger of air attack ever present despite the escort of three squadrons of ME 109s above them, the pilots did not delay.

They braked their machines, turned off the main landing direction and stopped while the men jumped out from the doors on to the grass with their kit, and ran across to the assembly point near the control tower. Then the pilots taxied at once down to the far end to take off alongside the path of the others still landing. It was hazardous, but less so than staying on the ground.

Meindl welcomed the Divisional Commander, exclaiming:

'It's a pity we couldn't have put you all into Hawkinge. It's much nearer Folkestone. But at least I've commandeered a certain amount of transport.'

Parked near the control tower were a random assembly of buses, Morris vans and private cars.


Once again, Pearson-Smith and Brown heard the throb of aircraft engines passing over their heads. The Junkers' line of flight away from Lympne passed directly over their hideout. The day had started better than they had expected. During the night the rain had cleared and now the visibility was good again and there were signs of the cloud breaking up, with a fresh breeze to help it. The night had been eventful. For a start there had been the mysterious and unexpected arrival of Captain Fleming. He had been openly furious to find two members of the army mixed up with his secret auxiliary Unit. It seemed to Pearson-Smith that he regarded them as the next best thing to a German patrol. Nonetheless he admitted that the prospects of Pearson-Smith and Brown making their way across country undetected, through German lines and back to the regiment at Mersham, was slight.

'You should have broken out last night,' he remarked scathingly. 'In this game you take time by the forelock. No opportunity presents itself twice. Anyway you have no option but to move by night.'

He then thought a bit and suggested:

'At least you could get in communication with your regiment and bring some fire down where we need it behind the lines. You could do that from the other end of the wood here.'

So, with undisguised reluctance, Pearson-Smith and Brown had crawled out of the hideout into the wet grass before dawn and made their way on their bellies among the brambles and fallen leaves, to a point where, using the one inch map, they judged there would be a reasonable chance of making contact with the regiment whilst still remaining concealed. Their first calls went unanswered. Perhaps the regiment was not yet on net, or perhaps it was on another frequency. It was normal practice to change frequencies at least once every twenty four hours. At 0700 they tried again, laboriously going through every frequency mentioned in the signal diagram and at last, at 0720, they made contact.

'Don't at any cost give your location, even in code,' Fleming had warned them.

So Pearson-Smith merely said that they were unable to state their exact position but could observe various features. Fleming had also warned him to keep the messages short since there was a chance that the Germans would have the necessary equipment for locating hidden radio sets. Privately Pearson-Smith doubted how much use he would be, since the wood had been chosen for concealment, not for an observation post.

When the Junkers 52s started flying over, some with engines throttled back for landing, others obviously at full power on take off, Pearson-Smith realised his chance. It would hardly matter if the fire was not adjusted exactly onto the target. With that number of aircraft milling around anything would do. He gave the grid reference of the control tower and ordered a regimental target. Five minutes later he and Brown heard the first explosions from the airfield.

Meanwhile, with a coolness that amazed and worried Pearson-Smith, the farmer had put on his ordinary clothes, crawled out after them and set off openly across the stubble fields from the end of a nearby hedge. His intention apparently was to go home to his farm, look after things, have a cup of tea and take a quiet look at what was going on.

'He's taking a bloody great risk, he is.' Said Brown.

Two hours later he reappeared.

'How'd you get on?' asked Brown.

'That shelling's let all hell loose,' said the farmer, 'and there's quite a lot of traffic on the road. They've commandeered cars, trucks and buses. If I were you,' he went on, 'I'd get some fire down on the roads from Lympne down to Hythe and round by Newington. That's where they seem to be going.

Then he went back into the hideout to talk to Fleming again.

Pearson-Smith and Brown studied the map and decided on Newingreen crossroads, but the reply to their call for fire was yet another message about a move to a new location. The regiment was being forced to retreat further and further by the German advance. They crawled back to the hideout and sat in one corner feeling like unwanted relatives whilst snatches of whispered conversation reached them. One fragment of Fleming's was:

'If he comes in today he must come in to Lympne. It's the only way. They're bound to fly him in. That's when we've got to get him.'

Pearson-Smith wrapped himself in a blanket against the chill underground damp and feigned sleep, then did doze off.

Further west at Bexhill, the German 34th Division was forcing its way out of the town north. They had already joined up with the 26th Division who had made fast progress across the flat, marshy ground, of Manxey Level and were now driving up towards Herstmonceux supported by artillery that the horses had difficulty handling. They pressed north up into the wooded low hills characteristic of that part of Sussex, leaving behind the dilapidated, salt-laden, summer villas of Pevensey and Bexhill. The going became progressively more difficult. The stretches of wood seemed endless. Even so, some companies leading the 34th Division nearly reached the battlefield of 1066 where William the Conqueror defeated King Harold. They came in sight of that long shallow valley beneath the huge stone bulk of Battle Abbey where the fate of England was decided nine hundred years before. Then at midday, a strong counter-attack by the British 42nd Division breaking out from the Winston Line near

Heathfield and driving down past Herstmonceux backed by the resources of two other brigades, one armoured, forced the two German divisions to recoil and concentrate on defending their centre. A vicious battle developed between Windmill Hill and Boreham Street, just north of the Manxey Level. The British attackers had almost reached as far as Horse Bridge across the river when they were finally held, a mile short of the Lamb Inn on the Pevensey to Ninfield road.

News of the battle came back to the Canadians at Heathfield, comfortably ensconced in the grounds of Heathfield Park, and in, the Belgian lady brought coffee to the Brigadier and his staff who had occupied her drawing room and study.

'I have just been listening to the French radio. Of course it is German controlled. They say that they now occupy the whole of Kent and Sussex and they are setting up a provincial administration in Tunbridge Wells. But we are still here, are we not?' She smiled at the officers.

'Some SS man called Heydrich is to be Reichsprotector. Reinhardt Heydrich. Ugh! What an evil sounding name. And now you must excuse me, I must return to the kitchen.'

'Hell, war sure does have its compensations,' remarked the Staff Captain.

'Not for much longer, I guess,' replied the Brigade Major. 'One always gets moved from good billets, and there's quite some battle going on round Pevensey.'

The Canadians were, if anything, slightly ahead of the Winston Line which grew more defined where it followed the A265 road east along the ridge towards Burwash and Etchingham. The diminutive River Didwell twisting alone the valley south of the road made a natural obstacle and there were troops ensconced by Dudwell Mill and round Bateman's, Rudyard Kipling's beautiful old Tudor house that stands in the valley below Burwash. Miraculously the wrought iron gates between the stone entrance had survived the nation wide hunt for scrap metal that had stripped both town and country of gates and railings. So had the lead Tudor statues among the garden's neatly pruned privet hedges. The National Trust housekeeper persuaded the troops to keep out of Kipling's former home, but they occupied the stables and were dug in on the slope that runs north from the steep banks of the river.

At Etchingham, where the ridge ends and the squat tower of the ancient church stands close to the railway crossing, the troops had moved into houses and into the railway station. Indeed, that curious stone station looking for all the world like a little country house was scheduled to be the site of a major stand if the invaders did succeed in reaching the Winston Line. Since time immemorial the River Rother has been both a line of advance and a line of defence. At Etchingham it turns north to run in a gap between the hills which the railway line also utilises on its way to Tunbridge Wells.

The defences along the Rother displayed an ingenuity so remarkable as to be almost amusing. At Salehurst, three miles further down stream, a pillbox was disguised as a railway hut; another on the A29 below the Park Farm appeared from a distance to be an oast house. There was even one in front of the great square bulk of Bodiam Castle. The Castle itself was built in 1386 because the river was then navigable that far and so it was the obvious place for a fortress to stem the raiding parties of the French. Early in 1940 its carefully preserved ruins became an ammunition store for the Home Guard. Paradoxically, they used the great wooden doors of the south postern for target practice with their old Lee Enfield .303s, oblivious of the possible results if a bullet should happen to enter the castle and hit the stockpiled ammunition.


Further east towards Ashford the Winston Line followed no natural feature at all. But fortunately for the defenders, although the German 1st Mountain Division had taken Rye, neither it nor the 7th Division at Lydd and Camber had followed up the river's course along the traditional route. Like the troops around Pevensey they had been held along the line of the woods and hills. The 7th Division's tanks had run into unexpected obstacles. Not merely crossroads sewn with concrete 'dragons teeth', but girders and ditches and concrete obstacles of all kinds had delayed them at corners on quiet tree-lined roads. And every obstacle meant a few more casualties. Individual British soldiers had leapt from ditches and hedgerows to plant sticky bombs on the tanks' sides, apparently fearless of their action being suicidal in broad daylight. Inevitably one or other of the following tanks had shot the assailant, though seldom before a sticky bomb or a Boys grenade had successfully 'brewed up' the leading vehicle. There were some 60,000 Home Guards in Kent and Sussex and most were prepared to sell their lives dearly. Winston Churchill, in a macabre phrase, had urged them to 'take one with you'. Now many did.

Thirty miles away in West Sussex it was a more encouraging story for the defenders. General Sir Alan Brooke, long grateful for the response from the Commonwealth earlier in the year in sending troops half way round the globe to help the mother country, now ordered a further attack on the German enclave. At all costs the port of Newhaven, tiny as it was, must be denied the invaders. The quays from which the cross-Channel steamers used to ferry tourists to France in peacetime would otherwise see the unloading of less welcome cargoes – the tanks and heavy guns which Generaloberst Strauss' 9th Army must sorely need. But Newhaven had fallen during Sealion's first hours. Brooke allocated its recovery to the Australian Division, already stationed outside Brighton. Brooke's staff had laughingly worried about letting the notoriously hell raising Aussies loose among the traditional temptations of Brighton's fleshpots. In the event they barely had time for a pint of still unfamiliar bitter in the local pubs, let alone a night out. They were woken before dawn on the 23rd to be briefed for the Newhaven assault and by 1100 were proving themselves magnificently in a ferocious three pronged attack on the west side of the harbour.

The Lewes road provided one-approach route, though a dangerous one since it was under heavy fire from the eastern side of the river held by the Germans as far north as Beddingham. Indeed, it was a miracle that they had not taken Lewes. So the Australian Division forward battalions came in on the Rottingdean and Peacehaven road, over the hill by the golf course and down the steep slope past the hospital into the town. As their move across the hill was extremely exposed, the RAF were asked urgently for fighter support. One of the pilots was James Scott, now equipped with another Spitfire – and with very firm instructions to eschew 'victory rolls' under any circumstances. His mission this time was to strafe the east bank of the harbour where the German troops had consolidated fire positions among the cranes and the waterfront warehouses, and where they appeared to be preparing for the reception of cargo ships. Seeing once again the maze of narrow streets and the crowded old houses through which the Australians would have to fight he thought, 'rather me any day'. His walk out of Seaford had taught him just how laborious travel can be on the ground.

By fast movement and skill the Germans had managed to secure the old grey painted iron swing bridge that links the two sides of the harbour. The hundred-year-old construction, swung on pivots by hand, clears the way for vessels up to eight foot draught to reach the inner harbour. Here, coasters used to bring in coal and wine from Europe, unloading with the aid of six grey-painted turntable cranes of decidedly venerable vintage. The German Divisional orders had been explicit. At all costs these loading facilities, ancient as they were, must be captured intact and safeguarded. So must the bridge. The outer harbour was useful, particularly with the long new breakwater built of concrete just before the war and sticking out, as Scott saw it from the air, like a piece of lattice work into the sea, a lighthouse surmounting its end. But if Newhaven should prove to be the only port captured for some days the maximum use would need to be made of its facilities. In consequence, the company on the western end of the bridge was detailed to hold on at all costs.

The Australians, prudently, moved down the back streets below the coastguard's station and worked their way round, house by house, to the quay with its individually numbered wooden jetties. They could get no covering fire from the fort on the headland. Whoever had designed the gun emplacements and pillboxes there had made the unjustifiable assumption that they would only ever need to fire out to sea. It was this that had made the landing on the beach between Newhaven and Seaford so much easier for the Germans. Not one of the gun emplacements nor pillboxes gave a field of fire over that beach. Much less did they command the harbour directly. If the Australians wanted machine gun posts they would have to set up their own. They first took over a fisherman's store on the wharf. Additionally they established mortar positions all round the base of the hill from which they could shell the ends of the bridge and the Germans on the opposite bank. Not heavy mortars. The British were as anxious to preserve what they could as anyone. Just 2 inch infantry mortars whose bomb fragments would prove deadly to men in exposed positions.

The house to house fighting was relentless. Several German sections surrendered, appalled at the speed and ferocity with which the Aussies lobbed grenades and charged straight in after the explosions. By 1200 one Australian Battalion Commander had reached the Ark Inn on the quay-side. In the public bar, above whose window the Inn sign flapped, creaking in the breeze, he set up his two machine gunners. Others went into the landlord's bedroom. From here he could command the western end of the bridge at close range. One of his companies gathered in the shelter of the pub and the nearby grain hoppers. Then, as the machine gunners raked the bridge with fire and the mortar bombs exploded against its lattice work, another company made a frontal assault through the centre of the town down on the bridge, bayonets fixed.

Thereafter, it was only a matter of clearing up isolated platoons on the west bank. The German hold there was broken. Furthermore, the east side of the harbour was now under continuous fire. Any possibility of bringing ships in for unloading had vanished. Effectively Newhaven was back in British hands from shortly after mid day – the Australian Divisional Commander lost no time in preparing to follow up this victory by forcing the bridge across the Ouse further north at South Ease, so as to penetrate the flank of the German advance towards Lewes.

In a special Order of the Day, General Sir Alan Brooke congratulated the Australians on their magnificent fight. It would, he said, be an inspiration to all forces engaged whether from the Commonwealth or not. The Battalion's Colonel posted a copy up in the bar of the Ark Inn and then found himself slightly embarrassed when the local fisherman coming in for a celebratory drink insisted on standing all the soldiers there a round. He seemed completely unworried that the Germans were still on the other side of the harbour, and might counter-attack at any time.

'Well,' said the Colonel with a grin, 'Someone's got to show these Poms how to handle the bastards.'


For the Australians' antipodean cousins, the New Zealanders, matters went less well. Their Division, happily settled into Maidstone for some months past, had been hastily ordered to Folkestone on Sealion Day. The move was a gruelling one. Though fully equipped by comparison with those Divisions who depended on requisitioned Green Line buses for transport, the New Zealanders had been forced to travel via Canterbury and Dover so as to enter Folkestone from the east and avoid any possibility of being bounced by the German paratroops occupying the heights above. What to peacetime trippers used to be an hour and a half's ride had escalated into a full day's journey, the Bren gun carriers grinding forward against a tide of refugees, while the unfortunate battalions sent by train were so delayed by the bombing of railway junctions that they only reached the town after midnight.

The Division arrived to find the port installations it had come to defend already destroyed. Buckled cranes hung over the quaysides. Some had toppled over into the water, crushing fishing boats. Debris lay everywhere.

91

'What in the name of the Almighty has been going on here?' General Freybeg demanded when he saw it. 'Weren't these listed as reserved demolitions?'

The territorial sapper major from the 1st London Division stuttered an answer.

'I'm afraid there was a misunderstanding, Sir. We were told the Germans were in the town so we detonated the charges.'

It was scarcely surprisingly. The retreat from Hythe had flooded Folkestone with 'odds and sods' from a dozen battalions. Frequent fighter attacks and the devastating explosions when shells from the Cap Griz Nez batteries whistled in, had compounded the confusion. The police were endeavouring to cope with frightened residents, all the town's fire appliances could not deal with the conflagrations.

'From now on,' announced Freyberg brusquely, 'I and my staff give the orders here.'

During the night anti-tank guns were sited along the residential avenues that stretch towards Sandgate behind the Leas. The Leas itself, that grassy seaward facing promontory of stockbrokers' homes and still elegant Edwardian hotels was now dug with trenches in addition to the anti aircraft gun emplacements already there. By dawn the Division was 'well forward', concentrated in the west and north west of the town, ready for the onslaught by the 21st Regiment, now identified as the German unit advancing through Sandgate.

Unfortunately for the New Zealanders the 22nd Airlanding Division attacked through the back door, from the north east, the one direction regarded as safe. By mid day the railway station was in their hands. Crushed between the 21st Regiment, fortified by two of Meindl's paratroop battalions, and the 22nd Division, the New Zealanders were forced to withdraw along the coast towards Dover. They lost much of their equipment, but were lucky to escape with only a third of the Division killed, wounded or taken prisoner. By rights it should have been a massacre. Folkestone harbour fell into German hands shortly before 1400 hours. By 1500 hours engineer detachments had begun clearing the quays.

The news reached Captain Bartels in Dunkirk as he was holding his briefing for the sailing of the second wave of the invasion. From the moment his steward woke him with coffee and apologies at 0800, after a bare three hours sleep, September 23rd had been a day to remember – the wrong kind of day. First there had been Vize Admiral Lutjens' signal for a report on the previous night. Before that could be done he had to inspect Dunkirk harbour. Small coastal freighters, hit by bombs, lay resting on the bottom, decks tilted and tall funnels awash. Elsewhere only a gap in the line of vessels indicated a sunken barge. Yet loudspeakers went on trumpeting the music of the Engellandlied – 'Wir fahren gegen Engelland'. Bartels would have liked to stop the music, whether Dr Goebbels favoured the song or not. Worst of all were the grins on the faces of those French stevedores.

By lunchtime the report was complete. It concluded: 'We must acquire adequate unloading facilities on the English coast. Despite the success of early trials, unloading across beaches is impracticable in all except the most favourable wind and sea conditions.' As he signed the document, Bartels reflected that to conduct trials on the beach at Le Touquet had been loading the dice too much in their own favour. It was too gentle, too easy. And even so he remembered that on these exercises some of the barges had come to grief far out.

The word of Folkestone's fall came as he was lecturing his leutnants on the characteristics of the Hythe beach.

'Good news,' he told them, reading out the message. 'Now we can plan to take the heavy stuff across with some certainty. But we shall still need barges for the infantry and you'll still have problems on those beaches.'

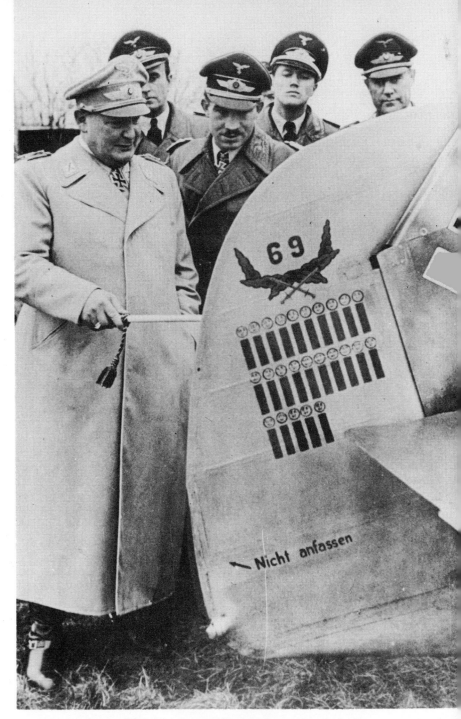

Nicht anfassen

Reichsmarshall Herman Goering inspects Oberstleutnant Adolf Galland's ME 109 fighter at Wissant on the French coast.

*Above* Commodore Friedrich Ruge, in charge of German minesweeping
operations for Sealion, with Admiral Lamprecht, summer 1940.

*Below* The Luftwaffe's aerial survey of Britain and the army's handbook
for 1940 with Hitler's portrait as a frontispiece.

*Above* Trials for Sealion at Rugen. Schwimmpanzer III is lowered into the water. It will then crawl ashore, obtaining air through the hose.

*Below* Schwimmpanzer fitted with pontoon floats on trails for Sealion.

British identification poster 1940.

# ENEMY INVASION.

---

## WHAT YOU MUST DO.

Remain at work: when unable to do so and you have no invasion duty

### CONTACT YOUR LOCAL WARDEN.

He will arrange for you to help the City to carry on.

If you are in Civil Defence, that is your job.

If you have no invasion duty, stand firm.

Do not leave your district; do not block the roads.

Do not listen to rumours; only obey orders given by the military, police, Civil Defence personnel or Ministry of Information.

Be on your guard against Fifth Columnists.

Apply to your local Warden for more detailed instructions.

Keep by you a 48 hours' supply of food and water.

---

Issued by the Birmingham Invasion Committee.

P30780 9B P)

Birmingham poster instructing civilians on what to do in the event of invasion.

*Above* King George VI inspects Essex Local Defence Volunteers (Home Guard) 20 July 1940

*Below* Prime Minister Winston Churchill visits beach defenders 31 July 1940

*Above* Scots Fusiliers practice defending East Coast cliffs 19 July 1940

*Below* Coastal artillery firing practice, 1940.

*Above* Dannert wire fences in July 1940 on the deserted Sandgate seafront—one of the intended Sealion invasion beaches.

*Below* Local Defence Volunteers training at Bisley June 1940. Both rifles and uniforms were scarce.

*Above* 6 inch guns on the coast at Shoeburyness June 1940—but in many places there were none.

*Below* Anti-tank obstacles blocked coastal roads. 'Molotov cocktails' would have set attacking vehicles on fire.

*Above* Some of the two thousand river barges assembled in French ports for the invasion.

*Below* Feldmarschall von Brauchitsch, C in C of the German Army, discusses Sealion preparations with senior officers on the French coast.

*Above* All kinds of fishing craft were pressed into military service for Sealion.

*Below* The invasion fleet under way on a preparatory exercise for Sealion.

*Above* German troops are debriefed after an invasion exercise. August 1940.

*Below* Rubber boats would be used for the Sealion landings during the final stages.

Defender and invader. *Above* This one was in Northern Command. Britain used dummy soldiers because real troops were over extended in 1940.

*Below* German SS troops prepare for the assault.

*Above* Armoured vehicles practise for the Sealion landings.

*Below* Converted Rhine barges were not ideal assault craft.

*Above* Bicycles (and also horses) were vital to German troop mobility in 1940.

*Below* Sealion plans put light artillery ashore in the first wave of the landings.

*Above* Throughout July and August German troops practised on the French beaches for the Sealion assault.

*Below* Germans ashore on British soil: German troops, directed by a British policeman, marching through St. Helier, Jersey on 23 August 1940.

# Chapter Five

## *1400 hours to 1900 hours – September 23rd*

For the commanders of the Luftwaffe's air fleets, Feldmarshall Kesselring with his Air Fleet 2 advance headquarters at Cap Gris Nez and Feldmarshall Sperrle with Air Fleet 3 further south, the second day of Sealion was as demanding, if not more so, than the first. By the time darkness fell the Luftwaffe would have logged another 1500 sorties by fighters over the beachheads, another 300 bomber sorties, another 160 Stuka sorties. The strain on the pilots was beginning to tell. For one thing, the RAF persisted in its attacks on the Channel ports and on German shipping although each raid brought more RAF losses. Five Wellingtons, six Blenheims, three Hurricanes and two Spitfires had all been shot down either by flak or by the Messerschmitts in attacks on Calais airfield and on Wissant. Yet always the Luftwaffe paid a price. St. Omer was out of action for four hours, Lille for four, Wissant for three, while the burning wreckage of Stukas, Heinkel III's and Messerschmitts testified to the proficiency of the RAF's bomb aimers.

Major Adolf Galland returned from a brief visit to Kesselring's Cap Gris Nez bunker to find one of his two beloved ME 109s, those with the Mickey Mouse on the fuselage and the laurel wreathed scoreboard on the tail, a mere skeleton. Its undercarriage had collapsed, its propeller blades were twisted and it had caught fire. A bomb must have fallen almost immediately behind the trailing edge of the starboard wing, digging in to the grass and then throwing the whole Messerschmitt clear up in the air as it exploded. Squads of French workmen were already filling in the craters under the direction of one of the Feldwebel. Nonetheless, it would be a good two hours before Wissant was serviceable again. Fuming with impatience, Galland walked around the dispersal. Finally he decided to brief his pilots immediately on the mission with which Kesselring had just entrusted him.

'Tonight, as well as giving cover to the second echelon leaving Calais, we have a particular mission of our own. I want four volunteers.' He glanced around at the group of pilots standing in the fitful sunshine in their flying kit.

'The trip is not dangerous,' he went on, 'In fact, to use that RAF expression it should be "a piece of cake". The risk lies in what happens if you fail.'

The pilots looked back at him intrigued.

'It is a simple escort job, a milk run across to Lympne. All you have to do is see one Storch safely landed at Lympne after dark.'

'What is the catch, Herr Oberstleutnant?

Galland's face beneath his peaked hat at its usual jaunty angle remained impassive. Did his mouth twitch a little under the pencil-line moustache? He knew that few of his pilots had any liking for the SS. The Schutzstaffel. Their silver skull and crossbones cap insignia had real meaning. The elite units of the Waffen-SS were officially 'the Fourth Arm of the Wehrmacht', equal in standing to the Luftwaffe, the Kriegsmarine and the army. They wore dark green. But this man belonged to the original black uniformed arm of the SS.

'The passenger,' said Galland still unsmiling, 'for whom we are providing an escort is SS Obergruppenfuhrer Reinhardt Heydrich. Volunteers please!'

By tradition every pilot of the JG 26 always volunteered for any task. This time Galland sensed a wavering. There was little doubt that some of them would rather shoot down an SS General than escort him. After a few seconds all the pilots in this particular group stepped forward.

'Thank you gentlemen,' said Galland. 'I appreciate your loyalty.' He chose four and then said brusquely:

'If this airfield isn't serviceable and in front line condition again by the time he arrives, we shall all be out of a job. Now, get on with it.'

The transfer of the newly appointed Reichsprotector from German to English soil was an assignment of the highest priority, albeit a minor job compared with the innumerable operational demands now being made on the Luftwaffe. Thus the fleet of Junkers 52 transports, originally 750 strong but severely depleted by the losses both in the original parachute assault and earlier in the day at Lympne, had to take to the air once again in the afternoon. This time their mission was the air re-supply of the 7th parachute division. The army was dependent upon the Kriegsmarine for their supplies. But the paratroops lived and fought on a much lower scale of supply than armoured or other formations, and the Luftwaffe looked after its own. Six hundred tons a day had been the requirement for an infantry division in the French campaign. The 7th Fliegerdivision reckoned to fight on half that amount. By evening, more than a day's re-supply had been dropped onto Hawkinge by the Junkers 52s. Generalmajor Meindl now had all he needed for his planned breakout to cut the Canterbury/Dover railway line. And tomorrow more would be unloaded for Loch's 17th Division.

The Führer had ordered more bomb attacks on London that night. The Führer's orders had the highest priority, naturlich. But they did not stop Grand Admiral Raeder's increasingly persistant requests for the air support that Goering had promised before Sealion was launched. The Sealion operational directives had stated that one third of the Luftwaffe's effort would be devoted to helping the Kriegsmarine keep the Channel clear for the invasion barges. In practice, over ninety per cent of the Luftwaffe's strength had been devoted to air and land targets in the south east.

At midday the Grand Admiral had insisted that further attempts should be made to locate the Home Fleet. With the headquarters of all three services now situated comparatively. close to each other for the first time since they had left Berlin, a proximity specifically ordered by the Führer himself as Supreme Commander, it became increasingly difficult to take no notice of the Navy's demands. Reluctantly the Luftwaffe Chief of Staff, General Hans Jeschonnek, ordered a take off time of 1600. To bolster his reserves he ordered the Luftflotte 5 under General Stumpff in Norway to contribute as many aircraft as it could. Stumpff had about a dozen coastal and naval cooperation aircraft that could be used as bombers or for minelaying. For weeks they had been continually occupied in attacks on shipping and dock installations in the north of England and in Scotland. Now they were allocated a sector of the North Sea for their search. So, in what Jeschonnek regarded as a truly desperate move, were the remnant of the Italian squadron participating in Sealion.

This squadron was the Italian dictator Mussolini's contribution to the subjugation of Britain. There was a story behind it, though not one that amused either Jeschonnek or Goering. Following the publication on the 9th of September of highly optimistic Luftwaffe figures for RAF losses and their own successes, Mussolini had begged the Führer to allow him to participate in Sealion. Hitler had refused, then conceded that a representative squadron of the Regia Aeronauticaa could join in attacking the RAF stations. The next evening this unit of twenty five three-engined Savoia-Marchetti 79s arrived at the airfield of Villa-coublay near Paris, although much to the annoyance of the German authorities. For a week the Luftwaffe created difficulties, finally refusing to service their machines on the grounds that they were all suffering from 'irreparable engine breakdowns'. However, when Hitler decided to launch the all out attacks on London that immediately preceded Sealion, the administratative fiction of unservicability was miraculously removed. The Italians were permitted to bomb Chatham on the afternoon of the 19th, losing one plane. The following day, again escorted by ME 109s, they flew twice; once against the City of London and once against the port. Despite the shooting down of two British fighters by the Messerschmitts, seven more of the three-engined Italian bombers were lost. The wreckage of one was examined by the British. It was found to contain, according to a journalist's report, 'no maps, but a lot of cheeses and Chianti'. The newspaper story quickly filtered back to Germany. Jeschonnek was furious. However, he now had little option but to order the remaining seventeen Savoia-Marchettis into action.

No-one at the headquarters was surprised when the Italians re-appeared at Villacoublay shortly before dark, complete with all seventeen aircraft, but having found nothing. They had scoured the waters off East Anglia.

'Niente,' explained their leader to the Villacoublay Station Commander. He held his hands wide in a great gesture, 'Niente, niente.'

Jeschonnek was rather more surprised that General Stumpff's aircraft had equally found nothing.

The truth became available to Grand Admiral Raeder before it reached Jeschonnek. The Home Fleet had been turned round off East Anglia and sent back north. The fate of the cruisers earlier in the day had decided the Admiralty that, for the moment at least, they should not risk their battleships in an area where the certainty of air attack was so great. The ships suited for the job were the destroyers, motor torpedo boats and the small patrol vessels, in all of which the Royal Navy had started with a tremendous superiority over the Kriegsmarine. There were fifty seven destroyers available even without removing others from convoy duty, against the Germans' ten. And three heavy, plus fourteen light, cruisers as against the Germans' total complement of the heavy cruiser *Hipper* and the light cruisers *Nurnberg, Köln* and *Emden*. Even the previous day's losses did not alter this balance substantially. Even more important, it was evident that the RAF was holding its own. At Storey's Gate Churchill reluctantly agreed to this change of plan.

It was the light cruiser *Köln* that had brought news of the change to the Germans. Following her original orders of September 21st she was still patrolling in the North Sea. Her 15cm guns, mounted in three turrets, were effective weapons. But she lacked one advantage that many of the British ships now had –

radar. The same pioneering in the practical application of radar to military operations which gave the RAF's fighter controllers such an advantage over the Luftwaffe, was also supplied to the Navy. All the battleships and battle cruisers carried it in elementary form. So did *Coventry* operating out of Portsmouth, so did *Berwick*, *Norfolk* and *Arethusa*. It was a Leading Seaman on HMS *Revenge* who first noticed the blip on the screen made by an unidentified ship twenty miles off in the North Sea. The weather was clearing now, with patches of blue sky showing between the clouds and greatly improved visibility, thanks to the moderate south westerly winds. On *Köln's* bridge, a recently joined Ober-Fähnrich, Werner Schunemann, was receiving instruction on the duties of an Officer of the Watch. He was searching the horizon through binoculars when he saw smoke far off in a low trail. Earlier today it might have been mistaken for low cloud.

'Smoke, port, about 260 degrees,' he shouted.

'Where?' asked the commander, a Fregatten-Kapitan.

Schunemann pointed.

'Ach So! Bravo Schunemann'. He spoke into a microphone: 'Get a man up to the crow's nest. Schnell, Schnell. Observe port 260 degrees.'

Three minutes later the report came down from the young seaman aloft.

'Three capital ships steaming north.'

'What distance do you estimate, Schunemann?'

'Eighteen kilometres, nineteen maybe.'

'Out of range of the *Köln's* guns. In any case,' the Fregatten-Kapitan explained to Schunemann. 'Our job is to find them, not to fight them. That would be crazy. Now we must shadow them if we can.'

Seconds later a salvo from *Revenge's* 15 inch guns fell a bare quarter of a mile short of the *Köln*. Fountains of spray hung in the air then crashed back into the water. Helped by the radar, the *Revenge* had been watching this potential target for forty minutes. Like *Köln* she also had a seaman in the crow's nest. His identification was exact. With the certainty that there were no British ships in the area, the Captain authorised opening fire.

On *Köln*, the Fregatten-Kapitan had immediately ordered a turn to starboard onto a course that would take *Köln* out of range to the north east. The ship was barely turning onto the new heading when the second salvo burst around her. Schunemann saw the forward gun turret disappear on a cloud of smoke and sparks. The acrid smoke drifted into the bridge windows. When it cleared they could see there was severe damage to the forward guns in turret C. The Fregatten-Kapitan ordered full steam. Black smoke billowed from the funnels.

'On some occasions discretion is the better part of valour,' remarked the Fregatten-Kapitan to Schunemann. This is one of them.'

The *Revenge's* third salvo fell short. But already another one of the battleships had opened fire. *Köln* was lucky to escape with only her forward turret gone and her steering gear slightly damaged. Her radioed information on the Home Fleet's position was promptly passed to the U-boat packs.


Having received his re-supply and handed over Folkestone to Generalmajor Loch's troops, the commander of the 22nd Airborne Division, Generalleutnant Graf von Sponeck, prepared for a break out towards Canterbury. He called the battalion commanders to his headquarters in the comfortable, though small, RAF Officers Mess among the trees by the side of Hawkinge airfield. He congratulated them on the success and speed with which their first task had been executed.

'Gentleman,' he said, 'It is now essential to paralyse the British effort further. Our next objective to cut the important railway line between Canterbury and Dover. Already the main line through Folkestone is denied the British. Now we must cut this link and encircle the port of Dover for its capture in turn.'

He glanced at a sheet of paper in his left hand and continued: 'We cannot disregard our casualties. Regrettably they are as high as they were in the operation in Holland. Of 6,680 men we have lost over 1510. I shall therefore retain one battalion of infantry regiment 65 to hold our base here, together with one battery of artillery regiment 22 and the anti tank company.'

The General now moved to a large map hung on the wall.

'Regiment 47 will use the transport already commandeered to move along this road.' He pointed to the B2060. 'I expect you to take Temple Ewell and cut the Dover to Canterbury road and rail lines not later than dawn tomorrow. The remaining two infantry battalions of Regiment 65 will follow the coast road to Dover.'

When the General had finished outlining his plan he turned to domestic matters and beckoned forward his Quartermaster, who explained various points such as that of the issuing of requisitioning slips for rations would be carried out by battalions. No German currency was to be used. All cars commandeered should at once be marked with swastika flags. If necessary, civilian drivers could be pressed into service.

The General took over again. 'Remember,' he said, 'All civilians who attempt to enter the area by passing road blocks are to be arrested and kept as prisoners of war. On our side, the taking of objects of any kind which are not absolutely necessary for the war, from private houses or land, constitutes looting, and looting is punishable by death.' The General concluded:

'As I said in Holland, while this division is operating in a foreign country the behaviour of every officer, NCO and man must be so exemplary that the honour of the field grey uniform will remain as unblemished as it was in the Great War. Anyone who violates this rule will be punished.'

Generalleutnant Graf von Sponeck was a meticulous man, a career officer with a keen sense of pride in the traditions of the German army. Other divisions might have different views. He personally doubted if the SS Adolf Hitler Bodyguard Division, due to arrive in this area in the second wave, would have the same code of behaviour as himself. For the time being, however, his word was literally law.


A few miles further west at Lympne airfield very similar orders had been given by Generalmajor Meindl. The airfield, however, was still in a mess at 1600 hours. Surveying it from the former controller's desk in the tower, Meindl swore gently under his breath. The air landing of the 22nd Division had been only a hair's breadth from disaster. He was still amazed that the British shelling should have started so promptly as the aircraft began landing. It had been a considerable gamble for the Junkers 52s to land at all. Now the wreckage of thirty one of them lay strewn at the sides of the airfield where they had been hastily cleared by his men. The control tower itself had no glass in the windows, but perhaps because it was so small, or perhaps by chance, it had not itself been hit. The clearing of the wreckage and taking away the wounded to the regimental aid post, which had been established in the village of Lympne, took several hours. Then Meindl had set one battalion to digging trenches for anti aircraft guns. Others had been ordered to rest for a period of at least four hours while he planned their next move. His aim was to strike north of Ashford without delay. Already his battalions held a substantial perimeter north of the railway and around Sellindge in an arc to Lyminge where their perimeter joined that of the 22nd Airlanding's. Meanwhile, General Loch's 55th Regiment had been making its way up past Aldington. Between the two of them they could take Ashford in a clean pincer movement within twenty four hours. The first pre-requisite had been re-supply. Meindl's airborne soldiers carried only two days rations and one days iron rations. The re-supply came in, blessedly, on time, the parachuted loads plummeting down efficiently close to the ground marker.

Meindl was briefing his battalion commanders when his newly appointed ADC brought in a message.

'An urgent signal, sir.'

Meindl read it and made no comment, calmly continuing his briefing. When it was over he turned to the ADC.

'And where in hell are we going to house the Reichsprotector?' he said.

'May I suggest, in the Castle, sir,' said the ADC.

'Ausgezeidchnet,' said Meindl. 'Proceed with the requisition at once.

'No need, sir. It has been vacated by the British army voluntarily.' He smiled.

'Good,' said Meindl. 'Then let us now deal with this unpleasant problem of the sabotage. How many civilians have been arrested?'

'Eighty-one in all, sir,' said the Adjutant. 'They are being held in one of the hangars.'

There had not been so many Home Guard in Lympne, naturally enough, as there were in Hythe. But those there were had been determined to fight. Where the road towards Aldington runs past the airfield there is a left hand bend among the trees. There, many months before, they had planted two steel tubes one at each side of the road protruding upwards some three and a half feet. They were rusty and set well back into the hedge. In consequence, no casual passer by would notice them. The Home Guards' intention had been to slot an iron barrier across the road into these two uprights. Somehow, someone during the day had stretched a steel wire between the two.

When one of Meindl's bodyguard came racing back on a commandeered motorcycle from delivering a message to the adjoining 55th Regiment at Aldington the wire had neatly beheaded him. The motorcycle had careered on churning up the mud and hit the hedge. The soldier's severed head, still in its steel helmet, rolled into the ditch.

As a result the entire male population of Lympne and the nearby hamlets had been rounded up and confined in one of the airfield hangars. The old gardener was among them. Meindl had instructed one of his English-speaking officers to question the group and ask if any would confess their guilt. There had been no answer except sullen looks from the men. Mass reprisals were not in Meindl's line. How much easier it is when one catches them in the act, he thought, gazing out over the airfield. There was also little doubt in his mind what Heydrich would order when he arrived and heard about it. He could hardly fail to hear about it. At the same time Meindl could hardly checkmate the inevitable vengeance by setting the men free.

'Have five kept as hostages,' he told the ADC. 'Release the rest to their homes.'


Pearson-Smith had returned to the corner of the wood. It was a bare two thousand yards from the side of Lympne airfield, though annoyingly the airfield was slightly higher up than the wood and he had no view of it. However, there was observation to the north west and down towards Aldington. Some German artillery had established itself a little way north of the village. Pearson-Smith guessed it must be pretty close to the location held by his own regiment only twenty four hours before. The risk involved in transmitting fire orders from behind the enemy lines was, to say the least, considerable. After some discussion with Brown they had agreed to take it in turns to man the set. After all, Brown was in fact as familiar with fire orders as anyone and he could read a map. Today at any rate there was a possibility of taking an active part in the fight. Once the front had moved on that possibility would disappear, they would quite simply be out of range of the guns.

'After all,' said Brown cheerfully. 'We're in uniform ain't we?' There's a thing called the Hague Convention, ain't there? They can't shoot us, they can only take us prisoner. Quite legitimate, that's what it is, quite legitimate, sir.'

Pearson-Smith was not entirely comforted by this justification for displaying courage. Furthermore, he had doubts about his own ability to tune in the radio, at least with anything like Brown's efficiency.

The extraordinary thing was that the Germans having conquered this piece of country seemed to be neglecting it completely. Pearson-Smith supposed that their occupation would be tenuous until they had captured their immediate objective. He remained, concealed in the edge of the wood, periodically making tuning and netting calls in as near a whisper as he felt would work. Finally, a little after 1400 he made contact. The regiment passed him their location in griddle but he could make no sense of the figures. Presumably they had changed the coding during his absence. They also expressed some surprise at hearing from him. He recognised the Adjutant's voice on the set, demanding, 'Send your location'. Laboriously, using the previous day's griddle, he composed the brief reply: 'No fear.' He passed through the co-ordinates of the guns he could see near Aldington. The first ranging round fell short. He ordered, 'add 400', then thought he heard an echo. The echo was repeated, louder. It said gutturally, 'Hande Hoch. Spion!'

Pearson-Smith looked up through the yellowing foliage to find himself face to face with the business end of a paratroop's Schmeisser.

When Pearson-Smith failed to return at 1500, the others in the hideout had forcibly to restrain Brown from going to look for him.

'If he's not come back, it's for good reason,' insisted the farmer. 'The risk in looking for him is too great. You'll have to wait until dark. Anyway, there are two others still to join us. Maybe they'll have some news.'


The only other German formation to obtain re-supply on this second day of Sealion was the Mountain Division at Rye. Down below the old town with its twisting cobbled streets, is the new harbour of Rye, hard by Camber sands. At high water very small ships can unload there. Usually it's only fishing vessels. Now Commodore Ruge had detailed part of his minesweeping flotilla to load and convey supplies to the jetties there. He couldn't spare many. There were fresh minefields to be laid west of Cherbourg to reinforce the screen of minefields named Bruno and Anton. But twelve of his thirty fast minesweepers able to carry ten tons each in cargo, succeeded in unloading at high tide in the afternoon, despite the risk of air attacks. Thus re-supplied with ammunition, and confident in its ability to live off the land, the Mountain Division prepared to push north to Bodiam and on to Hawkhurst, following the line of the Rother.

Nonetheless, as darkness fell on the 23rd, the maps at General Thorne's 11 Corps headquarters looked, from a military point of view, considerably more healthy than they had. Ranged against the ten German divisional signs spread between the various beachheads, there were now eleven infantry divisions, two armoured divisions, the First Tank Brigade and sundry others including the New Zealanders' and Canadians' independent brigades. Furthermore, information gleaned from the 2,400 odd prisoners so far taken revealed that the ten German divisions were far from complete. The two airborne, which had only forty per cent of the establishment of a normal division had been landed in full. But of the others, only perhaps half were actually on the ground. The rest would presumably come in the second echelon.

'It all depends on their second echelon,' Thorne told Brooke over the scrambler telephone at 1700 hours on the 23rd.

Brooke, speaking from the map room at Storeys Gate, reassured him obliquely –

'If the actions in hand succeed, then you will have little to fear on that score.'

'Pass my good wishes to the Navy,' said Thorne, 'Or is it the RAF''

In fact, Brooke was referring to the Navy. Yet unknown to him, fate had already taken a hand in Sealion. The weather, hitherto unexpectedly kind for this period of autumn, had now changed slightly. The decision to launch the second echelon had to be made by 1600 hours or 1700 hours at the latest. That is, if the assembled fleet was to make the crossing during the hours of darkness and not risk daylight interception by either the RAF or the Navy.

At 1600 hours the two Fleet Commanders were with Admiral Saalwachter at the Sealion naval headquarters at Wildungen. They had just been passed the weather forecast for the following twenty four hours. It predicted moderate to light westerly winds, variable later. Generally fine weather with local fog on the

English coast in the morning. Average temperatures. It was perfectly acceptable.

'The problem,' declared Lutjens, 'is the sea state and the wind at the moment. The wind is force 4, the sea state is 3.'

'The maximum the barges can take or close to it,' commented the other fleet commander, 'though no problem with tomorrow's forecast.

'Mein Admiral,' said Lutjens firmly addressing Saalwachter, 'you have read Captain Bartel's report. It's by far the best by any of those who accompanied the first crossing. He mentions the difficulties encountered with the tide, and particularly the losses resulting from attempting to unload in a sea state too rough for the barges. The conditions were the same then as they are now.'

Saalwachter turned to an aide. 'What are the exact numbers involved?'

'About 24,000 men, sir, but the important things are 900 tanks and the heavy artillery. They must go with the second echelon. So must the re-supply for the divisions already landed.'

The army colonel attached for liaison broke in.

'Mein Admiral, it is vital to get the Panzer divisions and the heavy artillery across. If the objectives are to be achieved the infantry must have armoured and artillery backing.'

Saalwachter reflected, then gave his verdict.

'Grandadmiral Raeder will have to make the final decision. Meanwhile, order the loading to begin. There is nothing to stop steamers going into Folkestone. No doubt your engineers will have cleared the quay-side by tomorrow.'

'Unquestionably mein Admiral', said the army colonel, whose brief from Generaloberst Busch was to persuade the navy to sail at all costs.


During the afternoon two waves of British ships were steaming into the Western Channel approaches, planning both to sweep the invasion lanes and to bombard Cherbourg, where, according to RAF reconnaissance reports, troops were assembling in large numbers. The obvious conclusion to be drawn from this was that a landing further west around Bournemouth or in Dorset was imminent. So by 1400 the 16th destroyer flotilla of nine vessels was midway between Plymouth and Cherbourg, followed by the cruisers Kenya and Nigeria and three more destroyers.

Inevitably they ran into the U-boat screen. A pack of five submarines were patrolling the waters between the Start Point and the Channel Islands, another six had been between the Scilly Isles and the Lizard. The famous ace, Kapitan-Leutnant Prien led the first attack. Squinting through his periscope, he identified two of the British destroyers as the K class, 1690 tons. Bare minutes later Prien had manoeuvred his position and his first torpedo struck HMS *Kashmir*. amidships. Another ten minutes later and one of the Tribals, *Mashona*, was hit. Both destroyers sank. Up on the surface the others raced in the routine pattern for anti-submarine work, firing the depth charges that exploded down below, throwing up great fountains of water. In the end Prien lost one of his pack, identified to the destroyers only by bubbles, and a growing slick of oil on the sea. Nor did this stop the progress of the British flotilla.

At Le Havre the German Vize Admiral felt compelled to order out all the strength he could afford to muster from both that port and Cherbourg. Three destroyers, the Zerstorers 6, 10 and 14 put to sea from Cherbourg, to be joined by six Type 35 torpedo boats and four Mowe torpedo boats. The Vize Admiral knew by instinct as well as reason that this might be the decisive naval encounter as far as Sealion was concerned.

The opposing sides did not meet until dusk. On HMS *Sikh*, another of the larger 1,870 ton Tribals, the Gunnery Officer stood in his director tower above and abaft the bridge. The tower was unenclosed. From it he peered through his optical rangefinder to telephone range and bearing down to the transmitting centre in the bowels of the ship, from whence his orders, converted into angle of elevation and bearing passed to the eight 4.7 inch guns. The calculation was not a simple one, involving as it did allowances for the speed of both ships and for the effects of wind and tide. There were still moments when the Gunnery Officer found himself amazed that they ever hit anything, particularly with the ship rolling as she was now in the swell. In the last light, at 1750, he obtained a clear sight of the Zerstorer 10 in the range-finder. On the forward gun platform the gun crew reacted instantly to the fire orders. One heaved the cartridge into the loading rack, another the fifty pound shell itself, a third rammed both home up the breech with his gloved right hand, the fourth slammed the breech block closed. Doing all that in seconds demanded co-ordination as well as muscle. A sudden shower of spray soused them as the gun fired with a tremendous crash. That was the snag about forward platforms, they were the wettest. Half an hour later, the flashes of *Sikh's* guns were illuminating the night, while overhead Junkers 88 bombers tried vainly to deter the superior British force. The gun crews, toiling in darkness, encumbered by their oilskins, were magnificent. *Sikh's* Gunnery Officer always reckoned it was her shells that sank Zerstorer 10. He'd had the benefit of the last daylight for his ranging. But it was not an argument likely to worry anyone. The action ended in a crushing defeat for the Kriegsmarine, with all three of their Zerstorers sunk and seven of the E-boats besides. The only thing the Royal Navy did not do was bombard Cherbourg. During the battle at sea fresh RAF reconnaissance photographs were developed that showed the earlier reports had been wrong. It seemed the Germans were garrisoning Cherbourg, not preparing for embarkation. In any case to have sent out a fleet of barges from there now would have been suicide.

At Dunkirk dusk saw Captain Heinrich Bartels wrestling with the logistics of the second echelon's departure. The port was partially clogged with sunken coasters, the barge crews were still tired. But, in the old phrase 'time and tide wait for no man'. If the weather calmed down, the second echelon would have to sail tonight. Bartels knew well how vital it was for General Loch and the other Divisional Commanders to receive the rest of their men, more supplies and above all, armour and artillery. Captain Erich Lehmann laboured similarly at Ostend and so did the Naval Station commanders at Calais, Boulogne and Le Havre. Somehow 500 guns, 900 tanks, 3,500 motor vehicles and a further 7,000 horses had to be transported, in addition to the 24,000 men. There were sufficient barges and steamers, despite the losses – just enough. News of the naval defeat off Cherbourg had yet to reach the other ports.

At Wissant, Adolf Galland waited for the Reichsprotector. The single engined Fieseler Storch, high winged and ungainly, stood by the hangar. No beauty, thought Galland, but you had to admit it could land anywhere. Lympne could be in bad shape, apparently the RAF had been raiding it constantly. But the pilot could put the Storch down in the small pool of light cast by the headlamps of a car. His own ME 109 escorts' main problem would be flying slow enough on the way across. His reverie was interrupted by the arrival of one of those great Mercedes favoured by the Nazi hierarchy. The driver leapt out and opened the rear doors. Out stepped a man of middling height in the black SS uniform. Galland saluted.

'Welkom Obergruppenführer.'

The man saluted. Galland suddenly noticed that his collar badges bore only the two silver oak leaves of a Brigadeführer, not the three of Heydrich's rank.

'Nein,' said the Brigadeführer, 'I am the Obergruppenführer's deputy. Henschelmann. The Obergruppenführer has been delayed.'

'Curious,' thought Galland, saying curtly, 'Your aircraft is here Brigadeführer'. No one worth their salt gave the courtesy of "Herr" before their rank, to SS officers.

A quarter of an hour later the Storch was airborne, with four ME 109s circling overhead, invisible through highly audible. At 1840 the deputy Reischprotector, the embodiment of the Third Reich's conquest, the personal representative of the Führer, stepped down on to English soil by the battered control tower at Lympne.

111

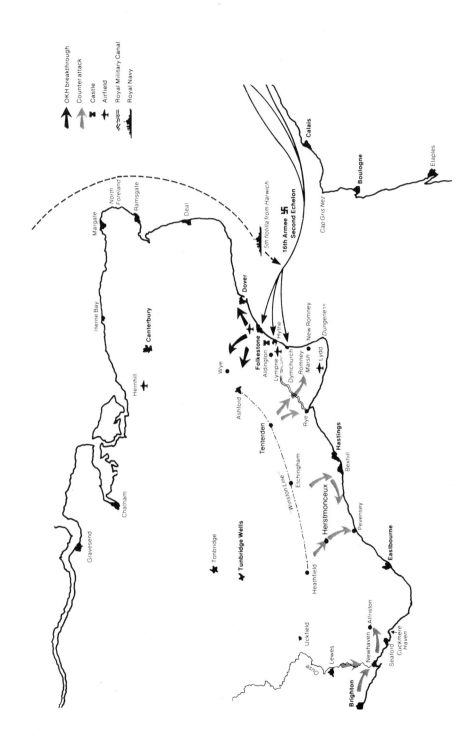

**Legend:**
- OKH breakthrough
- Counter attack
- Castle
- Airfield
- Royal Military Canal
- Royal Navy

Etaples

Boulogne

Calais

Cap Gris Nez

16th Armee
Second Echelon

5th flotilla from Harwich

Margate
North Foreland
Ramsgate
Deal

Dover

Hythe
Aldington
Lympne
Dymchurch
Folkestone
New Romney
Romney Marsh
Lydd
Dungeness

Herne Bay

Canterbury

Hernhill

Wye

Ashford

Tenterden

Etchingham

Winston Line

Hastings
Bexhill

Herstmonceux
Pevensey

Chatham

Gravesend

Tonbridge

Tunbridge Wells

Heathfield

Eastbourne

Uckfield

Lewes

Ouse

Newhaven
Alfriston
Seaford
Cuckmere Haven

Brighton

Rye

# Chapter Six

*1900 September 23rd to dawn September 24th*

The first Führer Conference at Ziegenberg was intended to be an historic moment. Hitler had a feel for such things. That was why he had insisted on the Armistice with France of June 22nd being signed at Compiègne in the same railway carriage as witnessed the signature of the 1918 Armistice, when Germany had capitulated. On that sunny June day he had danced a jig for the benefit of the photographers. The afternoon of September 23rd was also one for flashbulbs and cameras as the Führer's huge open Mercedes touring car drew up outside the headquarters. This was the day when the Führer descended from Felsennest to take personal command, the day when a Reichsprotector was landing on English soil as his Viceroy. The loudspeakers blared forth the Engellandlied as the Guard of Honour outside presented arms.

The Conference began at 1800, they would dine afterwards. Hitler sat at the map table in his usual simple uniform. He wore only his Great War Iron Cross, in marked contrast to the heavily decorated Generals surrounding him. At his left sat Goering, while Raeder, Von Brauschitsch and Keitel stood. In fact the complete German High Command had assembled for the occasion. The tall, strong faced, arrogant Generaloberst Keitel was the Chief of Staff of the Wehrmacht, the 'defence might', the German Armed Forces as a whole, outranked by Goering only because Goering was so much the Führer's confidant. In attendance were General Halder, the army Chief of Staff, von Rundstedt, Saalwachter, Kesselring and Sperrle. The 2nd Air Fleets fighter squadrons were on special alert in case, by chance, the previous day's unsuccessful attempt to raid von Rundstedt's headquarters was repeated here.

Inside the Führer himself opened the meeting with a characteristic dissertation on the historic victory now imminent. His eyes alight, his small moustache bristling, he told the Generals,

'There is mass hysteria in England. Roads are crowded with refugees. The British nation has lost faith in the warmonger
Churchill now that his second rejection of a generous peace offer
has been followed by intensified air attacks upon London.' Here
Hitler turned to compliment Goering. 'The efforts of the Luftwaffe in the last forty eight hours have been beyond praise.'

It was not uncommon for the Führer to explain the military
situation to his advisers. 'The enemy,' he went on, 'will be forced
to commit their destroyers in the Channel. They will suffer losses
rendering them unable to protect their convoys.' Now came a
sop to Raeder. '*Hipper* and *Scheer* will sink unprecedented ton-
nages in the Atlantic.' After a further half hour he concluded. 'At
all costs we must re-inforce Sealion's success.

This was the moment for which Raeder and the other Admirals had been steeling themselves. Tactfully they explained that
the weather at the moment was unsuitable for the barges to make
a crossing save at the risk of drifting seriously off course and
possibly being swamped. It was the conclusion Raeder had
reached with Saalwachter, though they spoke only of postponing the command to sail until later in the evening. Even so they
were unprepared for their master's fury. In the midst of it news of
the sinkings off Cherbourg arrived. Three destroyers and seven
torpedo boats lost. It was impossible, Raeder promptly declared,
to safeguard the western flank of the sea crossing tonight. All at
once the bitter inter-service pre-invasion arguments over the
length of the beachheads swelled up again. Originally the
Kriegsmarine had wanted Folkestone to Eastbourne as the
landing zone, against the army's near incredible demand for a
200 mile front from Margate to Lyme Bay in Dorset. On August
26th Hitler had settled on Folkestone to Brighton. Now the
Navy was evading even that responsibility. For von Brauschitsch
it was crucial to reinforce and re-supply all the landing beaches.

'By tomorrow night,' he told Hitler, 'the Divisions at Newhaven and Pevensy will be running out of ammunition.' Raeder
countered by demanding more Luftwaffe raids on the British
ships in Portsmouth. Goering observed that could only be done
if the Führer's continuing 'Grand Attack' on London was de-

creased. Predictably the Führer took this lead and ruled that 'the terror bombing must continue. It is as important a weapon as the invasion'.

When the Führer Conference broke up at 1930 the only decision reached was for the second echelon to remain at readiness, in spite of the need for it to have sailed by 2200 if it was to land at the following dawn. At Dunkirk Captain Bartels received the stand by message with resignation. In his opinion the sea state might improve, though not until the early hours.


Thirty miles away, across the Channel the newly arrived deputy Reichsprotector was inspecting his new quarters in Lympne Castle. He thought it unimposing and cramped by comparison with the grandiose castles of his homeland, not that he had ever been a guest in one. However the Great Hall, modest as it was, struck a chord in his nature with its high beamed ceiling. But the British had left the place in chaos. Annoyingly no one could find any of the Castle servants. Such a private establishment must have had them before the army moved in.

'Where are they?' he demanded. 'There must be a butler, cleaning women, gardeners.'

The paratroop hauptmann detailed as his liaison officer naturally had no idea. Until two hours before he had been concerned fully with the capture and subsequent defence of the airfield. Then he recalled the hostages temporarily penned in the hangar.

'They are probably among the civilians arrested after the sabotage,' he suggested.

'Sabotage?'

The Brigadeführer's reaction was instant. 'Where?'

The hauptmann recounted the incident of the wire across the Aldington road, adding that he had heard the 55th Regiment had suffered too. Down on the Romney Marsh the sentry on a small ammunition dump had been knifed and the precious shells blown up.

'Give my compliments to Generalmajor Meindl,' snapped the

115

SS man. 'Remind him that although we are of equal rank, security is a question for the Reichprotector's office. Have those arrested brought here at once.'

'Only five?' questioned the Brigadeführer, as the frightened labourers were frogmarched in and pushed roughly against a wall of the Great Hall.

'There is one more' said the officer. 'He claims to be an artillery lieutenant who became detached from his regiment. He was transmitting on a radio from a concealed position when captured. He was in uniform.'

When Pearson was marched in between two troopers he was the first to be questioned.

'So. You are a spy?' The Brigadeführer's English was good, if clipped. Pearson Smith tried to keep calm.

'I am a lieutenant in the Royal Artillery. Number 211887.'

'Papers?'

Pearson-Smith fumbled in his damp and creased battledress tunic. He pulled out a wallet and removed his identity card. The Brigadeführer looked briefly at it.

'Regiment?'

Pearson-Smith stiffened.

'Under the Hague Convention I am only required to give number, rank and name.'

'You do not deny that you were transmitting radio reports?'

'No,' Pearson-Smith conceded, 'I am an artillery observation officer.'

'In other words, a spy.'

'No!'

'Silence!' roared the SS man. 'The Führer has ordered that all Home Guards will be treated as saboteurs and shot. You are clearly not an ordinary lieutenant. You are too old. and you admit to spying.' He motioned the guards to take him away and turned to the civilian hostages.

'You might save his life if you reveal who are his accomplices.' Of the five three were farm labourers, one who was over sixty ran the sub Post Office, the fifth was partially disabled and kept chickens. After a long pause, during which they looked confusedly

116

around, one of the labourers volunteered.

'Never seen 'im before sir. Have we?' They all shook their heads.

'And the booby trap?' he demanded. Again only headshaking.

'Lock them up also,' ordered the Brigadeführer. He turned back to the table, opened a black briefcase and took out a roll of small posters. 'We prepared for this eventuality before the invasion,' he remarked to the hauptmann, handing over a poster. 'Have this nailed up prominently in the village at once.'

The poster was in English, though printed in German Gothic type which made it look foreign. It read:

### PROCLAMATION
*Unless information leading to the arrest of the saboteurs is received by the authorities the hostage from this village will be shot.*

*signed*        *Reichsprotector*

Barely five hundred yards away from the Castle two men were lying up in the wood. One was Peter Fleming, the other the anonymous farmer. Neither was in uniform. The farmer whispered:

'It wasn't easy. They've imposed a curfew. Luckily while I was with the gardener they went round actually ordering people out to read a notice at the Post Office.' His voice hardened. 'They're going to shoot the hostages if they don't get information about that wire we put across the road. That's a bastard, sir, just a bastard.'

Fleming gripped his elbow. 'You're trained, you're more valuable. I warned you it wouldn't be easy. Now, what about the gardener? Can he do it?

'He thinks some old cock and bull story about the ghost of a Roman soldier walking on the terrace might do the trick. Otherwise he'll tell the man there's fighting broken out down by

117

the canal. He's very game, sir.'

Fleming shifted his wrist cautiously to look at his watch, the fallen leaves crackled like fire when one moved. It was 1905.

'What time does the ghost walk?'

The farmer chuckled softly. 'Ten o'clock precisely. I chose that because moonrise is nine-thirty three.'

Overhead the few puffs of cumulus cloud had dwindled to nothing. It was already a fine night, though breezy. Shreds of fog were rising over the Marsh below, and curling up the steep field below the castle.

'Ideal,' commented Fleming softly, 'and with the moon in the last quarter there won't be much light for them to see us by.' Night sight OK?'

'Spot on,' said the farmer.

At this moment the drone of aircraft engines drowned all other noise. Bombs began to fall on the airfield.

'Let's get in position. I'll only open fire if you fail.' said Fleming. 'if he hasn't come out by midnight make your own way back.'

Very slowly the farmer began to work his way to the edge of the wood, closer to the Castle terrace, at either end of which sentries now stared upwards at the RAF Blenheims above. The guard commander had asked for a small searchlight, but none was obtainable yet.


The gardener had problems with the sentry at the stone arched entrance to the courtyard. Eventually an officer was summoned who spoke some English, then the hauptmann. The gardener, trying to stand straight in spite of his arthritic back, explained he had once been the butler. It was not true, but he knew where most things were stored.

'Butler?' the hauptmann did not understand at first. 'So, der Kellermeister. Gut. The Herr Reichsprotector will require wine for dinner.'

'I have the wine cellar key,' said the gardener, sadly. It had been entrusted to him when the owners left, with explicit instructions to keep the army out of the cellars at all costs. He hoped they would regard this as a special occasion.

'The Reichsprotector will dine at eight thirty,' ordered the hauptmann.

For the Fighter Command Headquarters staff at Bentley Priory, the days and nights had melted into one long timeless ordeal. Requests for air support from the army had poured in from dawn to dusk. September 23rd saw the prodigious number of over 1750 sorties flown in attacks on the German beachheads, but at the appalling cost of 97 more fighters shot down or damaged, leaving only 440 serviceable. Nor did the night bring relief. Hitler's Grand attack on London and other cities continued, so to a lesser extent did attacks on RAF airfields. Manston in Kent was in ruins, as it had been the first week of September. Tangmere, Middle Wallop, Biggin Hill and Kenley had all suffered. Air Chief Marshal Sir Hugh Dowding, forced to throw in his reserves in order to fulfill his one overriding aim of denying the enemy air superiority, felt that once again the exhaustion of his aircrews and the aircraft losses were bringing the RAF to breaking point. They had been close to collapse on September 6th, but were saved by the Luftwaffe's raids being switched from the airfields to the cities on the Führer's orders. As darkness fell outside, and the location of incoming bomber squadrons began to reach the Filter Room from radar stations and observer corps posts, Dowding remarked with a momentary weariness that alarmed his assistant

'Our one hope is that their losses break them first. What is the score so far today?'

'Over two hundred kills, Sir, and fifty one probables.'

In fact the Luftwaffe had lost 71 fighters, 30 Stuka dive bombers and 70 medium bombers so far during the day, though by midnight another 42 bombers would have been knocked out of the sky. Both sides inevitably exaggerated their claims. Often a single flaming wreck, streaming smoke as it spiralled earthwards, was thought by two, or even three, pilots to be their own individual victim. At much the same time as Dowding was making his appreciation, General Jeschonnek was doing likewise before rendering a report demanded by Goering for a resumed session of the Führer Conference at Ziegenberg. Checking the figures Jeschonnek commented acidly to his ADC.

'If these are right, the RAF has at most two hundred fighters left and is hardly flying bomber sorties. Yet they are at this minute raiding Calais, Boulogne and Cherbourg. It must be wrong. Assume a fifty per cent error.'

In his hastily drafted report, he informed the Reichsmarshall that overall RAF strength did not exceed four hundred aircraft. The Luftwaffe, despite losses, had 517 ME 109 and 154 ME 110 fighters, 634 medium bombers, 100 coastal reconnaissance and long range bombers, 521 Junkers 52 transports. This gave the Luftwaffe an apparent superiority of more than two to one in fighters and six to one in bombers. The over estimate was to prove crucial to Sealion's conclusion.


On the ground, General von Sponeck's break out achieved extraordinary success. His 47th Regiment out-flanked the re-treating New Zealanders by marching along the hills and de-scending on Temple Ewell before any serious defensive positions could be established. The Regiment seized the bridge that takes the main railway line over a minor road near the Abbey and was soon dominating the narrow valley in which the village lies. Both main routes into Dover were now under German control. although the other regiment, the 65th, was halted on the coast by a determined New Zealander stand at the Western Heights.

The paratroop regiments also breached the Winston Line, and partially attained their section of the Army Group A's ope-rational objective a good twentyfour hours ahead of schedule, though without real success. Their aim was to seize the Ashford Canterbury road and railway link, north east of the town. That meant breaking through the defending 24th Armoured Brigade, holding the Winston Line here. The paratroops did it by another forced march across country, capturing the village of Wye. But in the flatter land around the Great Stour river, which also flows from Ashford to Canterbury, they were halted. Among the London Divisions resources were a territorial battalion armed with forty eight Vickers heavy machine guns. These were posted at the river near Wye railway station and along the river line. Even with the aid of air strike by a squadron of ME 109's, the paratroops were unable to cross the river in daylight, while by nightfall its further bank and the bridges further down at Godmersham had been reinforced. Ironically this battle took place within a mile of Captain Peter Fleming's headquarters at The Garth, where there was considerable speculation as to his whereabouts. All they had heard from the Intelligence Officer was 'He's on a special mission that may take a few days.'

Elsewhere, however, the invaders began to suffer serious reverses. In the Newhaven-Seaford salient one of the tough Australian Brigades, the one held in reserve at the morning's assault on the harbour, went to join the British 45th Infantry Division at Lewes. Thus reinforced they began a night attack down the 27 road and the east bank of the River Ouse, forcing the Germans to recoil towards their original bridgehead.

At Old Heathfield dusk once again heralded change for the Canadians. As their Brigadier had forecast, a billet as comfortable as the Glen was unlikely to last. They bade farewell to the raven haired Belgian lady with genuine regret. She had told them little about herself, but their unabashed transatlantic questioning had elicited that her RAF officer husband was quite a guy, designed the bodywork for his own Rolls Royce, that kind of thing. Seemingly they had a Chateau in Belgium too which was now in German hands along with the Rolls. Yet she had insisted on cooking for the officers herself. Some lady. Two hours later she was forgotten in the sweat of digging trenches in the recently recaptured grounds of Herstmonceux Castle, a bare half mile from the German 26th Division forward line in the Pevensey beachhead. At dawn they would join the British troops in a second attempt to drive the Germans back to the sea.

The deputy Reichsprotector was pleased. The fumbling old servant had found candles and good Burgundy from the cellars though before being dismissed he talked a lot of nonsense about ghosts. Flames flickered in the great stone fireplace. It was a suitable setting for the Führer's personal representative, even if the food was disappointing. The paratroops were a rough lot and evidently cared little what or how they ate. Generalmajor Meindl, dining with him, even apologised for this fare. What more seriously concerned the SS man was the constricted size of the Occupied Zone that he had been despatched to take over. The German radio was announcing that all Kent and Sussex had fallen. Well, he accepted that some exaggeration was legitimate in the propaganda war. However he was surprised to find Ashford, Dover and Canterbury still in British hands.

'Get the maps,' he asked the hauptmann.

They spread them out on the oak table and, sipping brandy, Meindl indicated the breakouts now in progress.

'Are we in contact with Newhaven and Pevensey?' he asked.

'By radio. The situation in both seems confused.'

They talked for another ten minutes. Then Meindl, who was finding the heat from the log fire oppressive, suggested

'Let's get a breath of air.'

The three officers walked through the former drawing room and out through a door in the panelling on to the terrace. The sentries crashed to attention and saluted.

By the wood a shadow stirred. The farmer cursed under his breath. Three men. The one following must be the junior. He peered through the nightsight. Of the other two men, one was in a darker uniform than the other. That was it. The black uniform of the SS. The SS man stepped forward a pace to the edge of the terrace. The sentries were still frozen at attention. It was amazing how much you could see through the nightsight, it was as clear as the brightest moonlight. Very carefully he aimed at the SS man's chest, took first pressure on the trigger and fired. The gun made a low 'phut'. That was all despite the Hornet's high velocity bullet. The SS man staggered and fell. The farmer didn't wait. He wriggled quickly backwards into cover, twisted round, rose and walked back through the trees. He reckoned he must get across the other side of the Aldington road within five minutes.


At the resumed session of the Führer Conference at Ziegenberg, the debate on launching the second echelon continued. On the map room wall the clock showed 2150. It was von Brauschitsch who at last guided Hitler towards a decision.

'I accept the Grand Admiral's arguments about the western Channel waters. To repeat, the long crossing from Le Havre to Newhaven must involve unacceptable risk. But,' here the Commander in Chief leant forward, stubbing his finger emphatically at the map, 'We must never forget the Führer's guiding principle. "Reinforce success". At Pevensey and at Newhaven our Divisions are encountering heavy opposition. But at Rye the Mountain Division is pressing forward. We have just heard how both Meindl and von Sponeck are breaking out through the British encirclement. The fall of Dover is clearly a matter only of hours. We must utilise Folkestone harbour to reinforce that sector.'

Hitler nodded appreciatively.     'Mobilise all available steamers,' he ordered, 'And concentrate our U-boats and destroyers to defend the sealanes from Dunkirk and Calais.'

Goering broke in: 'The Luftwaffe will protect the invasion fleets,' he declared, 'My squadrons will provide continuous cover through the night.'

'And after daybreak too, I hope,' said Raeder.

Goering disregarded the Grand Admiral.

'I can assure you Mein Führer, their losses yesterday have crippled the Royal Air Force.'

Captain Bartels received the Führer's decision by telephone at 2230. Admiral von Fischel's Transport Fleet B, composed of the elements from Rotterdam, Ostend and Dunkirk was to sail again. So was a small proportion of Transport Fleet G from Calais. The rest of the second echelon was postponed for twenty four hours. As far as possible heavy equipment must be re-loaded on to steamers, which because of their 10 knot average speed, could afford to leave later in the night. That was all. The officer passing the message wished him godspeed. Bartels almost groaned aloud. It would be midnight before he had all the tugs and barges formed up off Dunkirk. It would be broad daylight when they landed. The only consolation was that the sea was reported calmer by the hour and the wind had already dropped to a mere breath over the harbour.

At Newhaven, the Generals commanding the German 6th and 8th divisions were in conference. They were discussing the tenacity with which the Australians were driving them back. Both formations had suffered heavy casulaties during the day.

'I have no alternative but to stabilise,' declared the General of the 8th, 'Until reinforcements arrive no counter-attack is feasible.'

'Let us hope they have a good crossing from Le Havre tonight,' said the General of the 6th.

When the Brigadeführer Henschelmann fell dying on the terrace of Lympne Castle, shot through the heart, it took Meindl very little time to react. Before the sentries had even appreciated what had happened, he was roaring:

'Turn out the guard. Search the slope down there.'

Captain Peter Fleming heard and understood the command. He pulled out a Mills grenade, holding the lever down and lobbed it with all his strength down the slope. Four seconds later its detonation gave the distraction he now wanted. As torches appeared on the terrace and paratroops began swarming down

124

the field, Fleming edged quietly back into his part of the wood. Three hours later both he and the farmer were safely underground in the hideout near Aldington.

'Congratulations,' said Fleming. 'Can't think why I came along, except for the fun I suppose.'

At the castle Meindl, not a man given to outbursts of temper, was openly furious. He ordered an immediate search of every house in the village. His paratroops would know what to do. To them a search meant a search meant a search. It meant ripping open mattresses with bayonets, pulling up floorboards, practically dismantling a house.

'What about the hostages?' asked the hauptmann.

'To be shot in the courtyard at dawn.'

'Including the so-called artillery lieutenant?'

Meindl hesitated. He sensed, with no way of establishing proof, that the over-age Lieutenant was connected with the sabotage.

'The Brigadeführer sentenced him last night,' added the hauptmann.

'He must be interrogated first,' said Meindl.

An hour later, when it was clear that the assassins would not be caught, Meindl decided to talk to this tiresome lieutenant himself. So Pearson-Smith was brought back again to the Great Hall, where the log fire whose heat had given Fleming and the farmer their chance, was now dying into embers.

'Sit down,' commanded Meindl. He proffered a cigarette and then shot out a question in his broken English.

'Your regiment is the thirty seventh, No?'

Pearson-Smith checked his surprise and nodded.

'Thirty seventh Field Regiment Royal Artillery,' he confirmed.

Meindl tossed a black leather wallet on to the table. 'Yours?'

Pearson-Smith nodded again. It had been taken off him thirty minutes earlier during an interrogation that was a lot less gentlemanly than this one.

'Bad security,' said Meindl accusingly, 'Never take personal letters into battle. That is bad. In the German Army you would be punished. So,' he went on 'you are an officer, not a spy.'

'Yes.'

Suddenly Meindl turned on him and roared 'Then where are you spending last night? How are your clothes dry in the rain? Answer.'

'I slept in a farmhouse.'

Meindl looked at him keenly. 'The Reichsprotector is dead. You will be treated as a prisoner of war. As a professional soldier I respect the Hague Convention. Also I respect the truth. In the morning you will show the hauptmann this farmhouse.'

# Chapter Seven

*Dawn – September 24th to Sunset – September 28th*

The five hostages were bewildered and terrified when they were marched into the courtyard of Lympne Castle. None of them had known anything about the sabotage, or the hideout, or the farmer's secret existence. The dawn of a sharp autumn morning was just breaking as the volley of shots rang out, scarring the old stone walls and echoing violently in the confined space. Their waiting womenfolk heard, still unable to believe that this nightmare was real. Through their sobs, the three labourers wives swore vengence for the Lympne martyrs if they could ever get it.

.In his locked room Pearson Smith prayed for the victims, though he was not a religious man. How incredible, he thought, that it was only forty eight hours since the invasion had begun. It seemed a lifetime. Up above in the tower a German sentry scanned the horizon as Pearson-Smith had done. It was going to be a glorious day, already the sun through the occasional clouds and patches of sky showed pale blue. But on the horizon the only silhouettes were of two destroyers, whose shells were bursting down below on the beach in innocent looking puffs of smoke. There were no lines of barges, no coasters, no motorboats. The second echelon had not arrived. Only far over to the east were a few steamers faintly visible.

'Franz', said the sentry in alarm to his companion. 'Something has gone wrong.'

During the night the barge fleets from Rotterdam, Ostend and Dunkirk had joined up successfully off Calais, and started their slow progress across the Straits of Dover. Both wind and sea had calmed to almost perfect conditions. Overhead the Luftwaffe flew continuous protective sorties. Zerstorer 20, her abortive role in the Herbstreise diversion over, had been brought

127

south to help the E-boats safeguard the eastern flank of the sea lane. But neither they, nor Admiral Doenitz's U-boats were able to prevent the 5th destroyer flotilla from Harwich moving down to the attack, albeit late because the RAF's reconnaissance reports the previous evening had indicated that the second echelon invasion fleet was not going to sail. But the fleet itself was late due to the indecision at the Führer Conference. As dawn broke, the great lines of barges were still ten miles off the English coast. It would take them between three and four hours to reach the furthest beaches, those of Dungeness. With the daylight came the destroyers and the start of a seaborne massacre, the gunners pumping shells at almost point blank range into the helpless barges.

In turn the fighter pilots flying above radioed for assistance. Virtually the whole of the Luftwaffe's remaining 634 medium bombers were on standby in fulfilment of the Reischmarshall's promise to the Führer. By 0700 nearly 600 of these were in the air, once again putting to the test the theory that ships were vulnerable to aircraft. The air battle developed swiftly as the RAF responded by throwing in all its available fighter squadrons. Nineteen of them were scrambled between 0700 and 0730.

James Scott was one of the pilots, conscious that the limitations of the Spitfire's range allowed him only thirty minutes over the area. One brief try at machine-gunning a barge convinced him that this was both difficult and purposeless; it must have caused casualties but it certainly didn't sink the barge. However, he did 'bag a Hun' before breakfast, one of the Junkers 88s bombing the British destroyers. So his score was evened up to 'thirty-all'. Flying back to Tangmere he thought of the letter he would write his aunt. For her it would be more than adequate compensation for the lost watch. He landed, hurriedly completed his report and was de-briefed. Then he walked to the mess for a late breakfast. The boy was sitting there at the end of one of the long mahogany tables.

'You're looking very pleased with yourself this morning,' remarked Scott.

For once the boy was shy. He reached out and gently put

128

something down in front of Scott. It was a little ½₂nd scale balsa wood model of an ME 109.

'I put the markings on before breakfast,' explained the boy, 'so it's finished.'

'That's beautiful,' said Scott. 'By the way, I finished a Junkers 88 off myself just now.'

'Did you?' said the boy. 'That's super.' Then he added 'I'm going to make a Spitfire next, I've got the plans.'

'Perhaps that'll make up for the one I crashed,' said Scott. And they both laughed.


The captain of the *Anne Marie* and his mate were again towing two barges, this time laden with tanks. They had repaired the tug's wheelhouse although they had lacked time to repaint the scars on the hull. It was of little consequence. At 0709 the gunnery officer on HMS Kimberley picked up the *Anne Marie* in his rangefinger. At 2000 yards the 4.7's could hardly miss. The second shell totally demolished the wheelhouse, killing both the captain from Hamburg and his mate. The third blew the *Anne Marie* clean out of the water, cabin, engine room and all. Minutes later the two barges she had towed were sunk as well.

The same scene was repeated again and again. Captain Bartels, this time not in his motorboat but on one of the steamers because he wanted to help organise the unloading at Folkestone, decided he must speak to the Fleet Commander. At 0745 he finally made contact on the ship's radio. Von Fischel agreed to his proposal. This was that since more British destroyers and MTBs must be expected from the Western Channel, the landings beyond Dungeness on Beach C should be abandoned. All the craft should make for Hythe and Dymchurch, with the steamers breaking away from the convoy and using their greater speed to reach Folkestone quickly.

Gradually the intensity of the German bomber attacks forced some of the British ships to retire. Two cruisers and four destroyers, all damaged, steamed back round the North Foreland. Yet the combination of naval gunnery and air strafing depleted von Fischel's fleet to a third of its numbers. Meanwhile the steamers fared better, losing only six out of thirty, but finding that the army's assurances on the readiness of Folkestone had been exaggerated. So thoroughly had the British sappers done the job of wrecking the port facilities that only two ships could berth for unloading at a time. Even though the flak guns landed on the first day had now been set up to anti aircraft protection round the harbour, there were further losses. During the day RAF bombers pressed home four major raids on the shipping, though they were apparently inhibited from bombing the town for fear of killing their own countrymen. When he finally got ashore, Bartels was appalled. Dunkirk was a haven of peace compared to this. He decided it was essential to see his old friend Generalmajor Loch and outline the naval situation to him.

At Storey's Gate the Cabinet Defence Committee met at 1000, spreading their documents out on the blue serge table covering. London had not been blitzed during the night and now the news from the front was good. First reports of the engagements in the Straits of Dover after dawn were already filtering through, enough to suggest a near disaster had occurred for Sealion. On land the German divisions both around Newhaven and around Pevensey had retreated marginally. Presumably they were now short of ammunition. Only at Ashford and Dover was the situation potentially menacing.

'Has the illustrious Reichsprotector taken up residence in Tunbridge Wells yet?' someone joked. The humour fell flat. Ugly rumours of reprisals for unspecified sabotage were reaching the Home Security network, whose South Eastern headquarters was indeed in Tunbridge Wells. However, the Prime Minister wound up the meeting in good spirits.

'I do not suppose,' he growled, puffing on his long cigar, 'that we are at the end of the road. Yet I have absolutely no doubt that we shall win a complete and decisive victory.'

General Sir Alan Brooke left Storey's Gate with firm orders to counter attack even harder.

Busch had delayed his sailing to England. Although his 16th Army held by far the largest bridgehead, it had seemed to his superior, von Rundstedt, that the move would be premature. When the morning's news reached von Rundstedt's headquarters he summoned Busch and the other army commander, Strauss, to see him.

'There is no point in mincing words,' he said.

The failure of both the Kriegsmarine and the Luftwaffe to secure the means of crossing the channel had prejudiced what had been an extraordinarily detailed and efficient plan.

'How long can your divisions last without re-supply?' he asked the two generals. Strauss replied that at the most he gave his divisions at Newhaven and Pevensey two days. Busch, knowing that a proportion of his second echelon had arrived, felt that Loch's 17th and the neighbouring 35th could keep fighting for several days at least.

'The worst problem is ammunition. Although the Luftwaffe can re-supply Meindl and von Sponeck,' he said.

Von Rundstedt interrupted him.

'But without more men they can hardly extend the bridgehead.'

Busch conceded that although the fall of Dover seemed likely, that was the most that could be hoped for.

'In that case,' declared von Rundstedt, 'withdrawal is the only sensible course.'

It was, however, not in Feldmarschall von Rundstedt's power to order withdrawal. When he accompanied von Brauschitsch to see the Führer later in the morning, they received a categoric refusal. Hitler's mind appeared to be dominated by quite minor considerations, like the assassination of the Deputy Reichsprotector, news of which had only just reached him. His fury at this was matched only by his disgust that the navy had been unable to fulfil the obligations he had placed on Raeder. He retained yet greater faith in the Luftwaffe's powers.

'The Air Fleets will protect the Bridgehead,' he assured the disbelieving Field Marshals.

That afternoon the Führer decided to quit the forward head-quarters at Ziegenberg and repair to the happier haunt of Felsennest once more. No sooner was he back than he was demanding over dinner that his aides produce the maps of the 'East Space', that great area of Eastern Europe and Russia in which he had seen the logical direction for the expansion of the Third Reich even whilst Sealion was in preparation.

Later that evening two of the staff officers of a Panzer division, due to cross to England in a few days time, were watching a film in a local French cinema. Suddenly a notice flashed on the screen demanding their immediate return to headquarters. When they arrived the Division's senior staff officer, a colonel, greeted them brusquely.

'Sit down, I have important news for you.'

'We are crossing to England immediately, are we?' asked one.

'Nein,' replied the colonel. 'The very opposite. We are to move immediately to East Prussia.'

Meanwhile, there were increasing signs of collapse at several places among the invading German Divisions. The Canadian Brigade, emerging from their trenches at Herstmonceux had fought their way for three miles down to the Ninfield-Pevensey road and by nightfall seized the cross roads by the Lamb Inn which commands movement across the whole of the Pevensey Levels. It is flat, wet land, broken up by innumerable streams and canals. As the Canadians took more prisoners they began to realise that their opponents were seriously short of ammunition. The better part of a company had surrendered at Grove Farm simply through lack of anything to fight with apart from bayonets and bare hands.

'I guess we're near the end of it, sir,' opined Sergeant Major Mackenzie to the Canadian Brigadier.

'Yeah, they've been ashore most all of three days now,' said the Brigadier, 'I guess an operation like this either succeeds in forty eight hours, or begins to fail.'

132

That night the Canadians linked up with the Duke of Cornwall's Light Infantry, out to revenge the cutting to pieces of their fourth battalion defending the Pevensey beaches. They had at last dislodged the Germáns from the western outskirts of Bexhill. The Intelligence officers estimated there were now approaching ten thousand men bottled up along Pevensey bay and the villages of West Ham and Pevensey.

It was the same at Newhaven and Cuckmere. The Armoured Brigade now held Alfriston firmly, having driven the depleted German 8th Division back into the village of West Dean and the surrounding wooded slopes. By nightfall the Exceat Bridge was in British hands again.

At Rye the Mountain Division who had received a small quantity of further re-supply through the medium of Commodore Ruge's minesweepers during the night, were in better shape. Yet they were in no condition to do more than hold off the continuing attacks which culminated in British infantrymen recovering Winchelsea at dusk. And throughout the day Dowding's fighters continued to strafe the beaches.

At Folkestone, Captain Bartels succeeded in finding General Loch, who had moved his 17th Division headquarters from the Imperial Hotel at Hythe into another similar establishment at Folkestone.

'Officially,' said Bartels, 'the whole second wave is still due to cross on time. But I can tell you that yours and the Mountain Division are the only ones to have received any part of the second echelon of the first wave.'

Loch nodded.

'Herr General,' Bartels continued 'I must advise you that in my opinion there is no hope of further reinforcement. You should prepare for an evacuation through this port using whatever shipping becomes available.'

At the headquarters of the 2nd Air Fleet in the Cap Gris Nez bunker, Feldmarshall Kesselring was also coming to conclusions. It was clear to him that the Luftwaffe had seriously over estimated the RAF losses and that air superiority could not be achieved in the short time left for Sealion to succeed. What he needed was an on the spot appreciation from a responsible officer. So at dusk the little Storch aircraft made another flight from Wissant to Lympne, escorted again by four of the ME 109's from Galland's Wing. This time it flew out empty and returned with one passenger – Generalmajor Meindl. This time the flight was more hazardous too. Lympne itself was now being shelled regularly by British artillery. Even the Storch with its astounding short landing and takeoff capability was lucky to get in and out successfully. Meindl's report to Kesselring was simple. The parachuting in of supplies remained perfectly feasible. The paratroops could continue fighting on this basis for many days. But the use of Lympne to fly in aircraft either for reinforcements of troops or for evacuation of them was out of the question.

After they had eaten, Meindl indicated that he would like to return to Lympne as soon as possible.

'That,' said Kesselring, his face set in an expression of clear distaste, 'is I regret, not possible. You are required to make a report to Obergruppenführer Reinhardt Heydrich on the circumstances in which his deputy was assassinated.'

Kesselring looked Meindl in the eyes.

'Was your security lax?'

'The situation was far too fluid for the establishment of a Reichsprotector,' said Meindl. 'And who in the name of heaven told him we were as far inland as Tunbridge Wells? It's one thing,' he commented bitterly, 'for Dr Goebbels to delude the world, another when he deceives us.'

'You can count on my support,' said Kesselring.


That night, after the last steamer had unloaded and Captain Bartels had sailed back for Dunkirk under such cover as the darkness afforded, General Loch decided that if the next dawn brought no further reinforcement of the other Divisions, they must conclude that Sealion was over and re-organise their perimeter to safeguard a withdrawal through Folkestone. It was a hard decision. All the signals received from Busch's headquarters ordered the continuation of the successful fight.


In the hideout near Aldington there was equally heated discussion on what to do next. The seventh man of the auxiliary unit had finally turned up, bringing word of the execution of the hostages. The villagers were in a state of shock. The paratroops house to house search had been ruthless and destructive. He had been extremely lucky to avoid arrest himself. It seemed the whole male population over the age of fourteen was again being rounded up and imprisoned in the castle, presumably in an attempt to identify the assassin. Fleming listened carefully. He knew there was an overall German plan to transport the whole able bodied male population to the Continent as forced labourers and to repopulate the island kingdom with 'Aryans'. It sounded preposterous, but the Intelligence boys believed it to be true. However that would hardly have begun so soon. This sounded more like a mass reprisal.

'It's out of the question thinking of rescuing them,' he said.

Finally the seventh man had seen a section of paratroops at the farmer's house with a British soldier. But they were in the distance, he wasn't sure.

'Must be Pearson-Smith,' said Fleming.

'I hope to Christ he doesn't give us away,' said the farmer.

Brown was outraged. 'I bloody swear he won't,' he shouted.

There was no doubt that these days in hiding were telling on all their nerves, thought Fleming, calming them down.


It was Reichsmarshall Hermann Goering, 'the fat one', as the fighter pilots called him, who talked the Führer into permitting a withdrawal. Like all empire builders, Goering was especially proud of his intrusions on other rulers' domains. His 7th Fliegerdivision was his private army. Its participation in Sealion had been worked out in Berlin and the details only revealed to lesser mortals like Generalmajor Loch in the final stages of planning. When Meindl's personal report to Kesselring on the situation reached the Reichsmarshall on the morning of September 25th he decided instantly that the paratroops must be saved. They had not merely fought magnificently. They were his – and Germany's – only parachute division. He demanded an immediate telephone connection with Felsennest. He already knew how the Führer's mind was now working, shying away from involvement with failures, regaling his imagination with conquest in the east.

'Mein Führer,' Goering argued, 'You have seen that the Fliegerdivision has been the key to rapid advance in Holland, in Belgium, in Norway. Now theirs is the only true success in England. You will need these men in Russia.'

Hitler agreed. A limited withdrawal could be made by steamer through Folkestone. Beyond that, the Sealion force must be sacrificed.


When the orders reached the paratroops at Lympne they could scarcely believe it. They understood little of naval matters, whilst further air resupply, admittedly in meagre quantity, had been dropped to them at dawn. They were in tremendous spirits. Yet now both they and the Airlanding Division had to carry out that most tricky of military exercises, a fighting retreat. The orders were specific. The infantry divisions were to concentrate on the corner of the Romney Marsh nearest Hythe, behind the barrier of the Military Canal, in preparation for embarkation at Folkestone during the early hours of the 26th. The airborne forces would secure this, Graf von Sponeck's men pulling back from their encirclement of Dover to hold the eastern approach to Folkestone, while the 7th Fliegerdivision manned the hills to the north west above Hythe.

A separate attempt would be made with the minesweeper flotilla to take off the remnants of the Mountain Division and the 7th Division from Rye Harbour. Already a British thrust from Tenterden through Appledore down on to the Marsh towards New Romney had all but divided the once continuous bridgehead in half.

For the last time, the Captains of the naval stations of Ostend, Dunkirk, Calais and the other Channel ports were supervising preparations for sailing to England. But this time the ships had no loading schedule. They would sail empty. Three fast crosschannel car ferries were unburdened of their cargo of seventy five tanks. They would be first into Folkestone. Altogether nearly eighty steamers were mustered, whilst Commodore Ruge allotted all his remaining twenty eight fast minesweepers to Rye. They could only berth at high water. Providentially the tide came up at 0535 and again at 1829, the first before dawn, the second after sunset. Ironically September 26th was the last day of the period the Kriegsmarine had considered suitable for launching Sealion.

On the evening of September 25th the German troops of the 55th and 21st Regiments quietly slipped back down the hills they had stormed, recrossed the canal and gathered shivering, company by company, on the Marsh. As they waited for the word to move on, and the shreds of autumn fog rose ghostly over the fields, sentries were startled by the eerie sound of laughter. Several loosed off shots into the darkness. The noise was the curious human sounding croak of the Romney Marsh frogs which inhabit the banks of the canal. It was to haunt those last survivors of Sealion until they finally surrendered.

Of the 90,000 men who had landed on September 22nd more than a third had been killed or captured by the 26th and of the remainder only 9,400 reached France from Folkestone while a further 6,000 were saved by minesweepers from the little Rye harbour quay. Both Loch and Graf von Sponeck were lucky. They got back. Despite the efforts of the Luftwaffe, the losses en route across the Channel were terrible. Of the thirty steamers from Boulogne nearly all were sunk. Since the final British total of men taken prisoner after September 25th was 32,341, as many as 15,000 may have perished in the chilly waters of the Channel.

Up at Lympne, the old gardener was one of the first to realise that the Germans had gone. Taking his courage in both hands, he stole round to the Castle and released the hostages. It took him a while to find Pearson-Smith, though. One of Meindl's last orders had been that as an officer he should be confined in a private room. Later, paradoxically, it was the slightly paunchy over age subaltern who pulled open the entrance to the hideout near Aldington and told Fleming, Brown and the others that it was all over, bar the shouting.

In fact some pockets of German troops held out until the 28th despite the leaflets the RAF dropped urging them to surrender. By then, Britain was returning to what in 1940 passed for normal, a wartime Britain of identity cards, ration books and one egg a week. The schoolboy just had time to finish his model of the Spitfire before the trains started running again and he had to leave Tangmere to go back to Herefordshire and those boring history lessons.

# The Defence of Britain 1940

*by Correlli Barnett*

On 27 May 1940, as the Dunkirk evacuation was beginning, and the panzer divisions stood on the French coast opposite the Straits of Dover, a sad flotsam of Belgian civilian refugees was passing through Victoria Station – people swept out of their homes and country by the onrush of German conquest. An Englishwoman acting as interpreter noticed that the policeman at her side grew more silent and pensive as the day went by. Eventually he confided to her the amazing thought that had struck him: "Why, Miss, this is really serious . . . This may happen to us."

In the months to come, after France capitulated, and the German sword swung its bloody point towards the English shore, this sense of amazement, of unreality, in the face of possible invasion and even occupation was universal among the British people.

Yet from 1588, year of the Spanish Armada, until the Great War invasion had been a recurrent British nightmare. In 1914 Kitchener held back two divisions of the British Expeditionary Force to guard the United Kingdom. Throughout the remainder of the Great War strong forces were retained at home for the same purpose. Yet after 1918 this ancient British fear of invasion died away completely; something which had never happened before, even during the long Victorian peace. The coming of Hitler to power in 1933 and subsequent British rearmament failed to re-awaken the fear. For in the late 1930s British attention was fixed not on the German army, but on the German Air Force. In the modern era, it was believed, a direct attack on this country would take the form of a "knock-out blow" from the air on London and other cities. The British army came a bad third in order of priority for re-armament.

It was only after the outbreak of the Second World War that British defence planners again began to consider the possibility that the Germans might land raiding parties somewhere on our vast coastline; perhaps even venture on a full-dress invasion. The existence of German airborne forces added a fresh dimension to an ancient problem. Nevertheless the danger still seemed remote enough. Under the inappropriately code-named *Julius Caesar* plan of October 1939, certain formations of the home forces were to be located within easy reach of the East Coast, ready to move against an invader; but otherwise little special preparation was put in hand.

But in April 1940 comfortable British assumptions were jolted by the successful German invasion of Norway in the teeth of British seapower. The enemy's readiness to run immense risks, to flout all sound canons of strategy as taught at Greenwich and Camberley, suddenly made the North Sea and the Navy seem far less formidable barriers. On 7 May the Chiefs of Staff discussed the dangers. They agreed that troops should be held near the main population centres in order to restore law, order and civilian morale in the event of a German inrush. General Sir Walter Kirke, the Commander-in-Chief Home Forces, pointed out that the Germans could not land heavy stores without first seizing a port.

The Chiefs of Staff agreed that the landward defences of our ports ought to be strengthened. Nevertheless, with Holland and Belgium neutral and France our ally, it was judged that only the East Coast stood in danger, since the passage of the Straits of Dover "would be a most hazardous undertaking and appeared to be an unlikely operation."

This comfortable assumption too was soon swept away. Just three days later Germany launched her offensive in the West. On 15 May the Netherlands capitulated, overborne by air-landings deep behind her water lines, her defence and civilian population confused and demoralised by widespread small parties of German parachute-troops, some disguised as Dutch soldiers or even, rumour was delighted to assert, as nuns. The fate of the Netherlands seemed to British leaders to offer a disquieting precedent. On 13 May General Kirke recommended that local defence forces should be raised to defend airfields and other key points against parachutists; what Winston Churchill resoundingly christened "the Home Guard" was born. Nevertheless the War Premier confided to the Chiefs of Staff his disquiet over the number of "trustworthy" troops in the United Kingdom, in view of the danger of German air-landings. Ditches were hastily dug across likely landing fields, or derelict cars strewn over them. Straight stretches of arterial road, tempting to pilots of Junkers 52 troop-transports, were adorned with steel erections like huge rose pergolas.

But it was the sensational German successes over the French army in the course of May and June which swiftly brought British leaders face to face with the danger of a large-scale German invasion. On 22 May, two days after Guderian's panzer divisions reached the Channel, the Chiefs of Staff noted that "the possibility of invasion on the south coast . . . creates a new threat, to meet which plans must now be prepared". On 25 May, the day before *Operation Dynamo*, the Dunkirk evacuation, began, the Chiefs of Staff submitted a report on British strategy should France be forced out of the war. On 29 May, with *Operation Dynamo* in full spate, the War Cabinet was warned by the Chiefs of Staff that the Germans might decide to stabilise the front in France in order to switch their attack to the United Kingdom. The British population, the COS pointed out, had not yet been alerted to the danger of invasion. The home army ought to be brought to the highest state of alertness. Beaches from Yorkshire to Newhaven ought to be put in a state of readiness.

On 6 June, the day after the Germans launched their final offensive against the French army along the Somme and the Aisne, the Joint Intelligence Committee reported that an invasion would probably open with the air-landing of 10,000 troops on the first day, if East Anglia was the selected place, or 20,000 if the Germans preferred Kent. On 7 June, as the French front began to break up, the Chiefs of Staff concluded that the likely sequence of an invasion would be: a. preliminary air offensive. b. preliminary naval offensive. c. airborne attack. d. seaborne attack. "But in view of Hitler's tendency towards the unorthodox and, therefore, the unexpected, it was thought possible that

141

seaborne invasion might precede or coincide with other forms."
Neutral Eire, wrote the COS, was a danger-point; the Germans
might seize it as a base for an attack on the west coast of England.
Troops therefore held in the West ready for use in Eire should be
Dominion formations "in view of Irish prejudices".

As June went on, and the French disintegrated from day to
day, the pace of British planning and preparation quickened. On
18 June, two days after Marshal Petain asked the German
government for an armistice, the COS were discussing arrange-
ments for evacuating 60 per cent of the populations of coastal
towns from Lowestoft to Hythe. They wanted a quick call-up of
registered age-groups in order to put more of the nation's man-
hood under military discipline, believing, as they put it, that
"there was a tendency for the danger of invasion to obscure the
danger of the breaking of morale through intensive bombing.
From the point of view of avoiding panic, the more men under
discipline the better". It was a pessimistic assessment of British
phlegm which the event was utterly to disprove.

Next day, 19 June, the COS warned the War Cabinet that a
danger now existed of air-attack or invasion. On 25 June the
armistice between France and Germany became effective. The
contingency for which the British had been planning ever more
urgently for some six weeks had now come about. Britain, alone,
was face to face with a triumphant and immensely powerful
Germany, who must finally crush her in order to wind up the
war.

A month earlier, on 25 May, the Chiefs of Staff had reported
to the War Cabinet on the British prospects of Britain repelling a
German invasion. Their conclusions were sombre: "should the
enemy succeed in establishing a force, with its vehicles, firmly
ashore, the army in the United Kingdom, which is very short of
equipment, has not got the offensive power to drive it out." In
view of enemy air power, the COS went on, we could not count
on the navy being able to operate in the southern North Sea or
the English Channel at all. In answer to a direct question from
the War Premier as to whether Britain could survive, the COS
answered: "The crux of the matter is air superiority."

The German victories in the West had doubly heightened the British danger. On the one hand the German armed forces now stood along the Channel coast, with Kent and Sussex within reach of their fighter cover; on the other, the British army had lost almost all its modern equipment in France – motor transport, field artillery, anti-tank guns, tanks. The 1st London Division, for example, responsible for the defence of the invasion coast from Sheppey to Rye, the key sector opposite the Straits of Dover, had only eleven 25-pounder field guns out of an establishment of seventy-two, plus four obsolete eighteen-pounders and eight 4.5" howitzers from the Great War. The division had no anti-tank guns at all, as against an establishment of forty-eight; forty-seven anti-tank rifles as against three hundred and seven; twenty-one Bren-gun carriers as against ninety; not a single Bren gun as against an establishment of five hundred and ninety.

In the whole of the United Kingdom there were only eighty "infantry", or heavy, tanks, and of an obsolescent pattern. They were all with First Armoured Division, and loaded on rail flat-cars at Aldershot ready for transhipment to an invasion front. The only other armoured division, Second, was equipped merely with a hundred and eighty light tanks, armed with no more than machine-guns, and virtually useless against German panzer formations.

Not only did the fifteen nominal divisions (excluding the returned BEF) in the United Kingdom lack striking power, they lacked mobility. The new C-in-C Home Forces, General Sir Edmund Ironside, reported on 19 June that each division had enough transport to lift one brigade. Motor-coach companies were being therefore organised. The British counter-stroke would arrive by Green-Line bus.

To equip the 471,000 men of the Home Guard, the country's static defence against air-landings, there were 100,000 rifles and 8,000 shot-guns. The C-in-C was however able to report that 75,000 Ross rifles were on their way from Canada, and that a million home-made "Molotov cocktails" were in hand. These petrol bombs were not the sole example of British ingenuity – or amateurism. To protect airfields, mobile pill-boxes were constructed, consisting of large concrete drain pipes up-ended on lorries and manned by Bren-gun crews.

Ironside, as C-in-C, faced an appalling strategic problem. With only under-strength, ill-trained, less than half armed, and largely immobile formations he had to defend four hundred miles of invasion coast, from the Wash to Southampton. Ironside himself – nicknamed "Tiny" since he stood six foot four inches high – was a fighting soldier rather than a brilliant strategic brain. In command of the allied intervention forces in North Russia in 1918-9 he had displayed leadership, energy and common sense. Now, in June 1940, he suffered from a lack of direct experience of German methods of Blitzkrieg. Trying to square what seemed to be the lessons of the campaign in France and the Low Countries with the desperate weakness of his own forces, Ironside drew up in great haste a plan, Operation Instruction No 3, for the land defence of the Realm. He presented it to the Chiefs of Staff on 25 June, the day the Franco-Armistice came into force.

According to "Operation Instruction No 3", there was to be a "crust" or outpost line along the coast itself to delay the enemy. Behind the crust there was to be defence in great depth stretching back to the heart of the country. "The general plan of defence," ran Ironside's Instruction, "is a combination of mobile columns and static defences by means of strong-points and 'stops. As static defence only provides limited protection of the most vulnerable points, it must be supplemented by the action of mobile columns." Since it was not possible for mobile columns to cover the entire area threatened, the Instruction continued, there had to be "stops" and strongpoints to hamper the enemy until the mobile columns could arrive. These "stops" – tank-traps, obstructions, water-obstacles, pill-boxes – were "distributed in depth over a wide area covering London and the main centres of production and supply. This system . . . will prevent the enemy from running riot and tearing the guts out of the country as had happened in France".

Finally, covering London and the industrial areas, there was to be a "GHQ Line", consisting of a continuous anti-tank obstacle covered by blockhouses and running from Yorkshire via the Wash, and the Cambridgeshire fens to the Blackwall Tunnel, and thence via Maidstone round the south of London. The main mobile reserves would be kept in groups behind the GHQ Line ready to launch a major counter-stroke once the principal enemy thrust had been identified.

Ironside reported to the Chief of Staff that the beach defences "were progressing well. All beaches on which landings might take place had been blocked and wired, and large numbers of anti-tank mines had been placed in position." The blockhouses covering the anti-tank (or GHQ) line were to be manned largely by Local Defence Volunteers (later dubbed the Home Guard); 'Molotov cocktails' – home-made petrol bombs – were to serve as their weapons against enemy tanks. To help remedy the acute shortage of armoured fighting vehicles, Bren carriers were being converted into light tanks, and cars and lorries into armoured cars.

Ironside's plan instantly provoked violent controversy. The Vice Chiefs of Staff expressed "the gravest concern at these dispositions. The coast was to be held only by a crust, and it appeared that the main resistance might only be offered after the enemy had over-run nearly half the country . . .". They believed that "the only policy was to resist the enemy with the utmost resolution from the moment he set foot on the shore".

The Chiefs of Staff themselves equally felt that there was too great a distance between the coast and the GHQ reserves, which would arrive too late. The War Premier weighed in with a memorandum pointing out that once the enemy got a lodgment, all troops elsewhere in the "crust" would be as useless as those in the Maginot Line. The coast should be held by "sedentary" troops. "Leopard" mobile brigade groups should be organised to counter-attack enemy landings within a few hours. Wrote Churchill: "All therefore depends on rapid, resolute engagement of any landed forces which may slip through the sea control. This should not be beyond our means provided the field troops are not consumed in beach defences, and are kept in a high condition of mobility, crouched and ready to spring."

145

Nevertheless the War Premier wrote that he agreed in general with Ironside's strategy, providing all possible field troops were stripped from the coast and grouped into "leopards". "The battle", he averred, "will be won or lost not upon the beaches, but by the mobile brigades and the main reserve."

On 29 June Ironside defended his plan to the COS. He pointed out that the majority of divisions along the coast were "only partially trained and had very little artillery"; therefore there was "little advantage in keeping larger forces for counterattack". Ironside told his colleagues: "If we had four armoured divisions in the United Kingdom, the whole problem of the defence of the country would be solved."

In retrospect the whole debate seemed unreal. So weak and immobile were the defending formations that it really hardly mattered what strategy they were formally committed to carry out. And indeed, after much discussion, largely on nuances of semantic interpretation of such words as "crust", Ironside's plan was approved.

The construction of all the ramifying "stops" and the GHQ Line itself was an immense undertaking. In June and July 1940 all the earth-moving equipment in the country, and 150,000 workmen under civilian contractors were busy at it. Steel and concrete anti-tank barriers began to burgeon under railway arches and on the approaches to bridges. Diminutive pillboxes appeared on embankments. Unfortunately the civilian contractors displayed poor tactical sense, and many of the pillboxes were sited in the wrong places, highly conspicuous, their loopholes looking in the wrong direction, and altogether highly dangerous to their intended occupiers.

It is as near certain, therefore, as anything can be in history, that if the Germans could have got a sizable landing force ashore in June or July 1940, they would have found the penetration of British land defences and the defeat of the British army hardly more difficult than brushing a way through cobwebs. All turned, as British leaders acknowledged, on air-power – on Fighter Command's ability to deny the Germans air superiority over the coasts and coastal waters.

But Fighter Command itself emerged from the Battle of France dangerously weakened. In the aftermath of Dunkirk the Command could only muster 331 Spitfires and Hurricanes. It is hard therefore to resist the conclusion that if the Germans had been able to launch their onslaught against the United Kingdom in July – air attack followed by invasion – Britain must have fallen.

Fortunately German unreadiness and indecision accorded the defenders a decisive respite. By September when the Germans were at last ready to launch an invasion, the British Home Forces had received over 400 more 25-pounder field guns from the factories; their stock of anti-tank guns had risen from 176 to nearly 500. The armoured divisions on which the defeat of enemy landing forces would so much depend now possessed nearly 350 medium and cruiser tanks, instead of eighty at the beginning of June. The coast defences had had two months' more work done on them. As early as 5 August, General Sir Alan Brooke, who had replaced Ironside as C-in-C Home Force on 18 July, was able to report that beach defences along the east and south-east coasts were well-advanced.

Brooke, an intellectual soldier with a penetrating analytical mind, who had commanded a corps in the French campaign with much distinction, abandoned Ironside's largely static strategy of a coastal "crust", "stoplines" and "GHQ Line". Instead, with the greater mobility and striking power now available to him, he proposed to contain German bridgeheads with local mobile forces; then smash the invaders in major counter-strokes by groups of armoured and infantry divisions held in reserve to the north, west and south of London. Nevertheless on 13 September Brooke confided to his diary that of his twenty-two divisions "only about half can be looked upon as in any way fit for any form of mobile operations".

But it was not a question of whether the home army by itself could defeat an invading force, but whether it could do so in concert with the Royal Navy and the Royal Air Force.

For the navy the advent of air-power posed a novel problem. No longer could the navy alone deny the sea to an invader as in

1588 and 1804. It was decided therefore that the action of the navy's light forces against enemy transports would be limited to the range of air cover provided by Fighter Command. The Admiralty had drawn up its broad strategy against invasion by the end of May. They hoped to attack the enemy by mines and bombardment before his invasion fleet even left its ports, providing early enough warning was received. If such an attack were not decisive, the enemy would be attacked on his arrival at the English coast. Since it was impossible to foretell exactly where the enemy might choose to invade, "our forces must be disposed to cover the area Wash to Newhaven as a whole". As a third alternative, the Admiralty contemplated "the happy possibility that our reconnaissance might enable us to intercept the expedition on passage".

The Admiralty reckoned that to fulfil their plans they would need four destroyer flotillas (thirty-six destroyers) with supporting cruisers. These flotillas would be based on the Humber, Harwich, Sheerness and Portsmouth. Extra destroyers and escorts were to be diverted from convoy duty to the defence of invasion waters. Moreover, the Admiralty at first proposed that the Home Fleet's battleships should come south from Scapa Flow to Plymouth.

These plans provoked vigorous protest on the part of the C-in-C, Home Fleet, Admiral Sir Charles Forbes. He argued that ships from his fleet could reach southern waters within twenty-four hours if need be; it was needless and dangerous to draw so much of British naval strength away from convoy protection and the battlefleet into the static protection of the coast. There is no doubt that Admiral Forbes took a less pessimistic view of German capabilities than the Admiralty. In July the First Sea Lord, Admiral of the Fleet Sir Dudley Pound, wrote that it was even possible that the enemy could land 100,000 men from fast ships without being intercepted by the Royal Navy, "in the hope that he could make a quick rush on London, living on the country as he went, and force our government to capitulate".

In the event, Forbes was allowed to keep his battleships, but most of the Home Fleet cruisers were dispersed in ports round the southern and eastern coast until the end of August. It was agreed that the battleships should only come south if German invasion transports were to be escorted by their heavy ships.

On 1 August the Air Staff issued a memorandum on the role of the RAF in repelling an invasion. In the pre-invasion period Fighter Command was to defend its own organisation and the aircraft industry against the Luftwaffe (in fact, it was doing so at that moment); Bomber Command would attack invasion shipping as soon as it began to assemble in enemy ports; Coastal Command was to keep enemy preparations under constant surveillance. Once the enemy began an invasion attempt, Fighter Command's first task would become to shoot down troops and tank-carrying aircraft, and to cover the Royal Navy in its attacks on enemy shipping. Bomber Command would hammer enemy ports and vessels at sea. Coastal Command would join Fighter Command in defending our own naval forces, and join Bomber Command in attacking enemy shipping with bombs and torpedoes.

Even Flying Training Command was to be thrown into the battle against enemy ships and beachheads. In June and July its 100-mile-an-hour Tiger Moth biplanes were fitted with racks for 20-pound bombs. As a last resort, German beachheads were to be drenched with mustard-gas from the air.

But where and when was the enemy intending to invade? British strategic guesses at first favoured East Anglia, with its open beaches and excellent tank country. Eire too was hotly tipped from time to time; even the remote north of Scotland. In August came a rumour via the British military attaché in Washington that the enemy proposed to land in the lightly-defended West Country, cut off Devon and Cornwall, and advance on London through the valleys of the Severn and the Thames. General Brooke regarded this report as highly unreliable.

Gradually the emphasis – and the weight of reserves – shifted towards the south-eastern promontory of England, where the sea-crossing was shortest, and where the passage and the beachheads would lie within German fighter protection. On 4 September, the Chief of Naval Staff warned that if the Germans "*could get possession of the Dover defile and capture its gun defences* from us, then, holding these points on both sides of the Straits, they would be in a position largely to deny those waters to our naval forces". The navy, he wrote, could do little to interfere with the subsequent German shuttle-service of supplies and reinforcements, at least by day. "I conclude therefore," glumly ended the CNS, "that if once we let the Germans get hold of the Dover defile and its defences, there might really be a chance that they might be able to bring a serious weight of land attack to bear on this country."

Next day the Chiefs of Staff themselves discussed the "vital importance" of the Dover defile, "the one part of our coastline where the full effects of our naval strength could not be developed". They decided that more ground troops were required right on the coast in this sector, in order to defend the heavy coast artillery on which "we relied for preventing enemy shipping reaching our shores".

Yet in September, as in May, the survival of Britain turned on the question of air superiority over the Channel and south-eastern England. The Luftwaffe had opened its bid for this superiority on 10 July, with heavy attacks on shipping in the Channel and on coastal towns. On 8 August it had launched its main offensive against south-eastern England, in the hope of bringing Fighter Command to battle and destroying it. Thanks to radar and the superlative efficiency of Fighter Command's control system, the attrition rate of the battle had remained consistently in British favour. But on 24 August the Luftwaffe began to concentrate on Fighter Command's airfields and the vital Sector Stations. By 6 September Fighter Command was in serious trouble, its efficiency more and more impaired by the damage or destruction of these Sector Stations. In a fortnight it had lost 295 fighters totally destroyed and 171 seriously damaged; whereas output of new aircraft was only 269. During the whole month of August the Command had lost 300 pilots, as against only 260 fledgling pilots turned out by the flying schools.

The Air Officer Commander-in-Chief Command, Fighter Command Air Chief Marshal Sir Hugh Dowding – an austere, taciturn, rather old-fashioned figure, affectionately nicknamed "Stuffy" by his young pilots – knew that if the battle continued like this, he faced inevitable defeat. And with air superiority at last in German hands, the way would be open for invasion. Dowding therefore decided that if necessary he would break off the battle, and withdraw the remainder of his fighters to the North of England. At all cost he must keep Fighter Command in being, whatever destruction the Germans wreaked over the towns of southern England. Then, when the German invasion was actually in progress, he would launch Fighter Command back into the battle to cover the navy and the army.

On 7 September the Director of Military Intelligence warned the COS that a German invasion was now very near. For two months, he recalled, the enemy had been building airfields in northern France, installing heavy guns round Calais, and collecting barges in southern North Sea ports. "During the last ten days," wrote the DMI, "these preparations began to approach completion and within the last day or two the stage has become set for possible invasion." More heavy bombers and dive-bombers were being concentrated in Northern France. There were now some 500 barges lying in ports from Ostend to Le Havre, capable of lifting 50,000 men and much of their equipment. Local inhabitants, on the French Channel coast, had been ousted from their houses, perhaps in order that the houses might be used to conceal invasion troops. Four spies who had recently landed in England had confessed that their purpose was to report on movements of British reserves in the area Oxford-Ipswich-London-Reading.

According to the DMI, "Considerations of tide and light conditions most favourable for invasion showed that these conditions would be at their best between the 8th and 10th of September. The most favourable conditions were believed to be a dark passage, half lift on arrival, with a rising tide." In his view, "the main attack would probably be made by barges covered by bomber aircraft escorted by fighters, and was to be expected anywhere between Southwold and Beachy Head".

That day the Chiefs of Staff held two urgent meetings, the

second presided over by Churchill himself, in his capacity as Minister of Defence. The meeting decided that "the possibility of invasion had become imminent and that the defence forces should stand by at immediate alertness". The Royal Navy had already put all its small craft and cruisers at immediate notice and stopped all boiler-cleaning. The RAF now moved from "Alert 2" – invasion in three days' time – to "Alert 1" – invasion imminent, and probably within twelve hours. The Army was already at eight hours' notice to move, and troops were standing-to at dawn and dusk. Although there was no intermediate stage between eight hours' notice and immediate action, it was now felt that eight hours' notice was too long in the present emergency. It was decided therefore to issue the codeword *Cromwell*. Unfortunately few recipients knew what *Cromwell* signified. When some units of the Home Guard heard of it (unofficially), they assumed it meant that the invasion was actually under way, and rang church-bells and blocked roads. In fact, *Cromwell* dated from Ironside's time as C-in-C, and was a merely warning order to take up battle stations.

British counter-invasion preparations had come to their peak. That same day, 7 September, the Home Secretary issued instructions that police were not to use or carry arms in areas occupied by the enemy, although they might try to stop small enemy parties not part of an occupying force from destroying property or spreading panic. The police were to control civilian evacuation where this was necessary, leaving a rearguard behind to keep order until the last moment. It had long ago been decided by the Cabinet that there should be no scorched earth policy in Britain, partly because it was hoped that there would be a short campaign and swift re-conquest of occupied areas, partly because civilian population not already evacuated was to stay put, and partly because the destruction of communications would prove as big a handicap to the defenders as to the attackers.

The Chiefs-of-Staff's discussions under Churchill's chairmanship in the late afternoon of 7 September were carried on to the accompaniment of a massive Luftwaffe attack on London. For, on the very edge of final victory in the air with their invasion preparations complete, the German leadership, stung by an RAF raid on Berlin, had made the catastrophic blunder of switching their attack from Fighter Command's Sector Stations to London. The Germans themselves had saved Fighter Command.

Once again, in the ensuing week, the balance of attrition swung against the Luftwaffe; the prize of air superiority which it had so nearly won slipped out of its hands. On 14 September Hitler postponed the invasion until the 17th. On the 15th Fighter Command won the biggest air-battle of the summer over London and south-east England, shooting down 60 German aircraft for the loss of 26 of its own. On the 17th Hitler postponed the invasion yet again; on the 20th the Germans began to disperse the invasion barges, of which more than a tenth had already been sunk by Bomber Command, to less vulnerable ports.

But for the British the invasion danger did not suddenly end; it gradually faded away. Might not the Germans still come under cover of an autumn fog? The British maintained their vigilance. On 18 October the Joint Intelligence committee reported that "a period starting on the 19th October appeared to be favourable. During this period the moon and tides were suitable, the incidence of fog likely, and Hitler's horoscope, a sign to which he was reported to pay considerable attention, was favourable during this period".

Horoscope or not, Hitler's mind was no longer on England, but Russia. Once more in its history the island had survived inviolate, its defences untested.

# The German Invasion Plans

## by David Shears

A minesweeper set out along the French coast one day in August, 1940, with some of the highest-ranking German Army commanders aboard. Field Marshal Walther von Brauchitsch, the Army C-in-C, General Franz Halder, his Chief of Staff, and others were being taken to observe a beach landing exercise conducted by German troops training for Operation *Sea Lion*, the planned invasion of Britain.

When the demonstration was over and the Army chiefs were returning to port, General Halder turned to the senior naval officer present and inquired: 'What do you think of the *Sea Lion's* prospects?'

The naval captain, now Admiral Friedrich Ruge, retd, was not the sort of man to be overawed by an Army Chief of Staff. He did not mince his words.

'Frankly, Herr General,' he replied, 'when I consider that as long as you plan to cross the Channel at a somewhat slower speed than Caesar's legions 2,000 years ago, I don't think much of it.' Admiral Ruge, recounting the story today, adds with a twinkle in his eye that General Halder was not amused and promptly changed the subject.

This anecdote illustrates a good deal of the background to Operation *Sea Lion* as seen from the German end: the Navy's scepticism of the Army's landlubber hopes of ferrying an assault force across the Channel in strings of wallowing river barges pulled by tugs at a speed of two to three knots. Looking back, few German officers of any Service would disagree with today's verdict of General Heinz Trettner – who was then a paratroop major – 'Thank God it was never tried.'

Yet, if we turn the clock back to that sunny summer of 1940, we can conjure up some inkling of the German mood. France and the Low Countries had fallen in one of the most brilliant campaigns of military history. Hitler had danced his jig and supervised the signing, on June 22, of the French capitulation in the Compiègne forest clearing where the Kaiser's generals had surrendered to France in 1918. He was not yet aware of how large a blunder he had committed when he had ordered Guderian's tanks to halt before Dunkirk on May 24, permitting the British Expeditionary Force to escape across the Channel. He was at the zenith of his career, confident of his military genius, exultant in his success.

Why did he not promptly order his triumphant forces to exploit their advantage and attack Britain by land, sea and air? He knew that the BEF had left practically all its equipment behind on the beaches and the refugee-clogged roads leading to Dunkirk. His soldiers were confident that if once they could set foot in Britain with adequate air support they would encounter little solid resistance. Yet weeks slipped by while Hitler went sightseeing in Paris and waited in Berlin or his Black Forest retreat for London to put out peace feelers. For the dominant mood in Berlin as well as in the Wehrmacht was that the war was virtually over. Despite Mr Churchill's defiant speeches, Hitler had nurtured from the start a kind of schizophrenia about the British and he still hoped London could be induced to make peace in return for German guarantees that the British Empire would be left intact.

But aside from these political doubts, which were only removed when the 'crazy English' rejected his so-called peace offer speech in the Reichstag on July 19, there were some practical problems. For one thing, there were no plans in the High Command of the Armed Forces (OKW) for an invasion of Britain. To be sure, the German Navy Staff had produced a study in November 1939 of the problems which any such operation would pose. It had listed two preconditions: naval and air superiority, and the Germans had neither. The German Army under von Brauchitsch had also produced a staff memorandum a few weeks later recommending a landing in East Anglia by 16 or 17 divisions including paratroops and a brigade of cyclists.

These preliminary studies were not plans in any true sense of

156

the word, and their authors conceded that they were only 'first thoughts'. Furthermore, Goering's Luftwaffe when asked to comment said that the practical difficulties were such that the whole idea of invading Britain must be rejected except as 'the last act of war against England which has already taken a victorious course'. And Grand Admiral Raeder's naval staff agreed.

Nor were there any landing craft worth mentioning. Raeder had asked Halder early in 1939, when the plans for the western *Blitzkreig* were being made, how long the Army reckoned it would take to reach the Channel coast. Halder replied – according to Admiral Ruge – that 'if we reach Boulogne after six months' heavy fighting we'll be lucky'. So Raeder saw no need to start building landing craft at that stage. He was concentrating on rebuilding the German Navy which was still hopelessly outclassed by the British Fleet.

Throughout the summer of 1940, the three months from late June to late September when an invasion of Britain might have been attempted, the Germans had only one heavy cruiser – the *Hipper* – three light cruisers and at most nine destroyers available. The *Graf Spee* had been scuttled in the River Plate, the *Admiral Sheer* was earmarked for convoy raiding in the Atlantic and all the other major warships had been damaged in the Norwegian campaign or were not yet in commission.

Britain for her part had 14 capital ships, five aircraft carriers, 16 heavy and 46 light cruisers, 180 destroyers and 54 submarines. The Home Fleet alone, based at Scapa Flow, boasted five battleships, 11 cruisers and many smaller vessels. As Herr Friedrich-Karl von Plehwe, a former Army liaison officer at the Naval Operations Headquarters, remarks: 'The intervention of the British fleet hardly bore contemplation.'

There was hope of flanking the sealanes across the Channel with mines and attacking the British fleet from the air and with coastal artillery. But the German Navy was not confident. As Admiral Gerhard Wagner, who was then in the naval operations staff in the rank of commander, told me at his retirement home near Hamburg: 'Goering boasted that his Luftwaffe would deal with anything that could fly or swim – but we never believed him.' And, of course, the outcome of the Battle of Britain showed that the Navy sceptics were right.

Incredible as it sounds, the German Luftwaffe was more or less debarred from flying over Britain for more than a month after the fall of France. General Adolf Galland, the famous German fighter ace, attributes this order to Hitler's political reluctance to 'provoke' Britain. Galland was then the German equivalent of a group captain, commanding nine fighter squadrons based in the Pas de Calais area. He still has his logbooks from those days, and they show that the ban on entering British airspace was not lifted until July 25, when his fighters escorted bombers in a raid on Dover.

By that time, as we have seen, even the Fuehrer had reluctantly concluded that Churchill was not bluffing and that Britain was determined to fight on. And, in fact, as early as July 7 Hitler had discussed with Count Ciano, the Italian Foreign Minister, the 'very delicate and difficult' problem posed by an attack on Britain. Ciano offered up to ten divisions and 30 squadrons as an Italian contribution to an invasion of Britain. Hitler tactfully declined.

Meanwhile the period of hesitation and lack of planning in the German High Command was drawing to an end. General Alfred Jodl, chief of the OKW operations staff and Hitler's personal adviser on military operations, had prepared a memorandum on June 30 entitled *The Continuation of the War against England.* This said that since German victory was only a question of time it was possible to economise in the use of forces and to avoid risks. Jodl therefore advocated air attacks on the RAF and the British aircraft industry, supplemented by a sea blockade of Britain's vital imports. A landing operation should only be attempted after air supremacy had been achieved. It would not be designed to inflict military defeat since this would have been achieved already by the Luftwaffe and the Navy; rather would it be a kind of mopping-up operation to 'finish off' a country already on its last legs. But Jodl hoped Britain would come to terms and make these military moves unnecessary.

158

Hitler nevertheless authorised concrete planning to begin and on July 2 an order went out to the three services from OKW saying that Hitler had decided that an invasion of Britain might be undertaken if certain pre-conditions – notably air superiority – could be fulfilled. Admiral Raeder reported to Hitler on the Navy's views. He said the naval blockade and heavy air attacks on ports like Liverpool should suffice to bring Britain to her knees. He spoke at length of the difficulties of an invasion, which should be considered only as a last resort.

The curious thing is that Hitler agreed. Although he felt supreme confidence in his capacity for fighting land battles, the Fuehrer had no stomach for amphibious operations. As one German admiral later recalled: 'Hitler used to get seasick just from looking at a naval chart.' In the euphoric aftermath of his dazzling *Blitzkrieg* through France, Belgium and Holland one might have been expected him to brush Raeder's objections aside. He certainly had no time for timorous commanders in a ground campaign. But he listened to Raeder and soon came to agree with the Navy's scornful rejection of Jodl's view (in a memorandum of July 12) that an invasion of Britain could be compared to a 'river crossing on a broad front'.

At that stage the landing project was codenamed *Operation Lion*, but the name was soon changed to *Sea Lion*. Jodl admitted that the operation would be difficult but said that if the landings were made on the south coast 'we can substitute command of the air for the naval supremacy we do not possess, and the sea crossing is short there'.

Having listened to Raeder, Brauchitsch and Halder, Hitler issued, on July 16, his famous Directive No. 16, which began: *As England, in spite of her hopeless military situation, still shows no signs of willingness to come to terms, I have decided to prepare, and if necessary to carry out, a landing operation against her. The aim of this operation is to eliminate the English Motherland as a base from which the war against Germany can be continued, and, if necessary, to occupy the country completely.*

Some German generals, notably Field Marshall Gerd von Rundstedt and General Guenther Blumentritt, his chief of operations, contended after the war that Hitler never seriously intended to invade Britain and that the whole thing was a bluff. But the facts do not bear out this claim. Admittedly, Hitler was never very enthusiastic about the project. His interest waned as he became more aware of the risks and his thoughts turned eastwards, toward the dream of unleashing his tanks against Russia and succeeding where Napoleon had failed. But for a period of two months, between mid-July and mid-September, the Fuehrer was serious enough about *Sea Lion* to assemble a huge invasion fleet at the Channel ports despite the considerable economic cost. For the invasion armada, as we shall see, consisted mostly of river barges and coastal steamers essential to German industry. Even after Hitler made up his mind to attack Russia – a decision he took by July 31 – he kept the *Sea Lion* project and its preparations very much alive.

Directive No. 16 laid down that the landing operation should take the form of a surprise crossing on a broad front stretching from Ramsgate to an area west of the Isle of Wight. Just how it could have been a surprise is a mystery – Jodl had warned in his memorandum four days earlier that strategic surprise was hardly possible.

Five preconditions were laid down in the Hitler directive for the success of *Sea Lion:*

1. The RAF must be so weakened that it would be unable to put up any substantial resistance to the operation.

2. Sea lanes to the landing beaches must be cleared of mines.

3. Dense minefields must be laid on both flanks of the Dover Straits.

4. Powerful coastal artillery must give fire support.

5. So far as possible, British warships should be pinned down in the North Sea and the Mediterranean.

From this point on, *Sea Lion* was in business. The three Services were told to plan accordingly and report back to OKW as soon as possible. But one of the great shortcomings of Directive No. 16 – the only OKW operational directive for a landing in

Britain – is that it did not provide for a Combined Operations HQ, in which all three Services would work together without constant reference back to their own separate commands.

It merely directed that all three Services were to establish their operations staffs within 50 kilometres of Hitler's planned headquarters at Schloss Ziegenberg, near Frankfurt-am-Main. But this in fact was not done, and there was no equivalent of General Dwight Eisenhower's SHAEF (Supreme Headquarters Allied Expeditionary Force) which planned and executed the Normandy landings four years later when the boot was on the other foot.

The Army's plan was as follows: Six divisions would cross from the Pas de Calais to land between Ramsgate and Bexhill, four divisions would come from the Le Havre area to land between Brighton and the Isle of Wight, and three divisions would set up a third bridgehead in Lyme Bay. Some 90,000 men would go ashore in the first wave, increasing to 260,000 by the third day. Airborne troops would assist the landings, and nine further panzer and motorised divisions would back up the assault troops. Altogether the plan was to put 39 divisions and two airborne divisions ashore. Heavy fighting was expected in southern England. The first objective would be a line from Gravesend to Southampton, including the North Downs. The second major objective was a line between Maldon and the Severn, which would leave London surrounded. Then London would be occupied and motorised divisions would strike northward to Liverpool and Glasgow in the west and Boston, Hull, Newcastle and Leith in the east, with mopping-up meanwhile in the Midlands. Brauchitsch reckoned the whole operation would be relatively easy, and thought it could be concluded within a month.

But Admiral Raeder's Navy staff viewed the whole enterprise with grave misgivings. They argued that it was out of all proportion to the Navy's strength, the Channel with its weather, fog, currents and tides might present the greatest hazards for the invasion fleet, expensive and time-consuming conversion of existing barges into landing-craft would be needed, neither minefields nor air support provided safe protection, especially since Luftwaffe sorties depended upon good weather.

The Navy followed this with a second broadside which came out flatly against trying to execute *Sea Lion* at all in 1940. This staff memorandum of July 29 noted that the Army wanted the first troops to land at dawn, two hours after high tide (so the landing craft would stay firmly beached) and after a crossing by half moonlight. These three conditions could be fulfilled only in the periods August 20-26 or September 19-26.

The first of these periods was out, the Navy said, because preparations could not be completed in time. The second was getting dangerously near to the rough weather spell to be expected in the autumn. Even if the initial landing were successful, the buildup of the bridgeheads would continue well into October. The frail invasion armada could not stand more than the gentlest of seas, and Germany could not bank on the use of British harbours since these could easily be blocked or sabotaged by the enemy. Moreover, even the combined efforts of the minelayers, the Luftwaffe, coastal artillery and U-boats would not prevent the British Fleet from breaking through and creating havoc in the motley invasion fleet.

Raeder used these arguments to plead for an invasion on a narrow front, stretching only from Dover to Eastbourne. He stressed that ships from Cherbourg and Le Havre would be exposed to attack from Plymouth and Portsmouth, and that the Luftwaffe would be unable to protect such a long front as the Army proposed. The Army, shaken by the Navy's objections, began to doubt whether *Sea Lion* was feasible in 1940. But Halder and Brauchitsch continued to press on with preparations, and their visits to the landing exercises on the French coast continued through most of August. Halder wrote in his diary on August 6 that 'the only driving force in the whole situation comes from us'. But he angrily rejected the Navy's plea for a short front. 'From the Army's point of view I regard it as complete suicide,' he told his naval opposite number. 'I might just as well put the troops that have landed straight through the sausage machine.'

While this Army-Navy argument raged on for weeks, the Luftwaffe remained blissfully unconcerned with *Sea Lion.* As we have seen, the air offensive against Britain had begun slowly. Goering had ordered his air force to move to airfields for the war against Britain. But in a meeting on June 21 he had told his commanders to use only weak forces against Britain until the start of the fullscale air battle ahead. Raids on land targets should be confined to the aircraft industry; otherwise the Luftwaffe should concentrate on destroying the RAF and attacking warships and convoys. Of course, all this was in line with *Sea Lion's* needs, but the Luftwaffe did not actually issue an operations order for the Britsih invasion until August 27.

By that time the Battle of Britain was well under way. At the beginning of August, Hitler had ordered the Luftwaffe to use all its resources to 'strike down' the RAF, its ground organisation and its supply facilities. The vicissitudes of this gladiatorial struggle of the skies are too well known to need repeating here. Its significance for *Sea Lion* is that the Luftwaffe not only failed to gain air mastery over the proposed sealanes and landing areas; it could not even prevent the RAF from bombing and straffing the invasion barges as they were massed in the Channel ports.

What a makeshift fleet that was! The reluctant Navy was mustering 2,000 barges from the Rhine and Holland, mostly without engines or at least incapable of making headway against sea currents without tug assistance. So almost all tugs of over 250 tons were withdrawn from German harbours. By September 4, the ports were clogged with 1,910 barges, 419 'tugs' – some of them mere fishing craft – 1,600 motorboats and 168 transport ships totalling just over 700,000 tons displacement.

By September 21, British air attacks, combined with long-range artillery and light coastal craft raids, had sunk 67 craft and damaged 173, according to German accounts. These losses were made up from reserves, but the improvised armada was considerably less seaworthy – at least so far as the barges were concerned – than the galleons of Philip II of Spain.

Throughout those tense weeks of August and September, when Britons watched the dogfights overhead and rejoiced at the inflated figures of German aircraft downed, planning for *Sea Lion* continued. A compromise was reached on the long-short front issue, and the Army's final plan, issued on September 14, was to force a landing between Folkestone and Worthing. It assumed that the invaders would be opposed by 17 British divisions, backed by 22 divisions as tactical reserves. (Early the previous month the German Army had estimated total British Army strength at 1,640,000 men, but this included 900,000 recruits, 100,000 men engaged in training and 320,000 trained men lacking proper equipment.) As time went on and the Luftwaffe visibly failed to measure up to Goering's boastful forecasts, the other Services grew increasingly sceptical – and so did Hitler.

By mid-September the Navy was complaining that the air war so far had not helped *Sea Lion* at all and 'in particular there is no sign of an effort to attack units of the British fleet'. The earliest possible D-Day for *Sea Lion* was put off from September 15 to September 21. But on the 17th Hitler postponed *Sea Lion* indefinitely. Everybody knew that it was as good as dead, although the order officially postponing it until the spring of 1941 was not issued until October 12. By that time, of course, Hitler had other things on his mind. He was yearning to invade Stalin's Russia and already laying plans.

*Sea Lion,* then, was never attempted. Despite rumours in southern England of blackened German Army corpses being washed up on British beaches after being scorched in seas of flame, and Germans never even attempted a small-scale landing on the lines of the Allied raids which preceded the Normandy invasion of 1944.

Most of the 'blackened corpses' stories were legendary. An American correspondent in Germany saw a hospital train full of men supposedly burned while testing asbestos suits, but the origin of this tale is a mystery. It is true that flame barrage tests were made along the Hampshire coast, with pipes carrying petrol to the sea, but no such system was installed until after *Sea Lion* had been cancelled.

The reasons were manifold: Goering's failure to win the Battle of Britain, the slow start due to Hitler's political hesitations and the unexpected speed of his western *Blitzkrieg,* lack of suitable landing craft, naval weakness, the blunder of Dunkirk. All these factors played their part, and no doubt the laurels awarded to the Royal Air Force are richly deserved. But military historians tend to underrate the naval argument that even if the Germans had achieved air superiority, the whole enterprise might have been ruined by a spell of bad weather. In other words, the strings of river barges to which the German Army was prepared to entrust its crack divisions were grossly unsuitable for a Channel crossing. The German Navy said they were only seaworthy in seas of up to Force 2 – which meant that one sharp squall could swamp them and send them to the bottom.

'They could stand nothing more than a light breeze,' said Admiral Ruge in an interview. 'I don't think they were properly tested for a cross-Channel operation. Of course, there were always barges chugging up and down the coast and the river estuaries – but only in calm weather.' Admiral Wagner described *Sea Lion* as an almost impossible undertaking. If the Luftwaffe had really been able to control the skies and keep the Royal Navy at bay, and if Germany had possessed 2,000 seagoing landing-craft with 12-knot speed – of the type later developed for the Mediterranean – *Sea Lion's* prospects would have been transformed.

But as it was, most surviving German officers today tend to share the scepticism the Navy showed from the outset. Even Army veterans like General Friedrich Stahl, an alert 85-year-old now living in retirement at Karlsruhe, acknowledge that it would have been 'an incredibly risky affair'. His task in 1940, as a staff officer of 16th Army based at Roubaix, was to ensure that the invading German troops would not lose their way on English country roads after the landing.

'If we had landed right after Dunkirk it might have been easier, but within weeks the British had removed their signposts – and we knew we were not going to get any help from the population,' General Stahl says. So his men produced 16,000 cloth signs; some with place-names already marked, others ready to be painted and hung up by pathfinders specially trained on British maps.

General Stahl concedes that he nevertheless wondered at the time how the Army would get across, and whether it would get any protection from the Navy and the Luftwaffe.

General Graf von Kielmansegg, latterly a Nato commander but then a young major in Germany's First Armoured Division based near Orleans, also began to have his doubts as the summer of 1940 wore on. But then, on August 28, he had no further need to worry about *Sea Lion*. He recalls that he was hauled out of a cinema that night and told to report to his Chief of Staff.

'As I entered his office I was sure that we were finally going to be told that *Sea Lion* had been given the green light,' he says. 'So I asked the chief of staff: "Are we on our way?" And he replied that I'd better sit down before he spoke. Then he said: "Yes, we're on our way but not to England – to East Prussia." So then we knew that *Sea Lion* was a dead duck.'

The young major was right. Hitler's fateful decision to move troops East, ready to invade Russia in *Operation Barbarossa* the following year, had killed *Sea Lion* stone dead. To be sure, the cross-Channel operation had never presented more than a slender chance of success. But with its demise Germany lost her only hope of delivering a quick *coup de grace*, of vanquishing Britain at her weakest moment. From then on, the only prospect of knocking Britain out of the war was by slowly strangling her sea lifelines. But neither the impending Blitz nor the Battle of the Atlantic succeeded in halting the rapid buildup of British strength.

By the summer of 1941, when the barges with their specially-fitted ramps could have been mustered again in the Channel ports, it was too late. Britain was far better equipped to repel boarders and Hitler's legions were fully engaged in his ill-fated Russian adventure. For Britain, it was a turning point; for Germany the turning point came the following year at Stalingrad.

# The Warlords

## by Alan Clark

In the summer of 1940 Britain was, in terms by which executive power is measured, as much a dictatorship as was Nazi Germany. Of course, it is true that the liberty of the citizens of Britain was of higher (although not much higher) quality than that of the Germans. But tactics, strategy, the allocation of resources – these were determined by one man, sometimes after consultation with a small caucus of soldiers and administrators, sometimes as a result of private inspiration.

The personalities of the two leaders – their moods and prejudices, their background and indoctrination, were of critical importance. Both Churchill and Hitler were warriors of genius. Alike unconventional, rebellious, with long periods of their career exiled in the wilderness, familiar with the extremes of public vituperation and acclaim, they were driven by burning and ruthless patriotism. They were inspired and had, to an extraordinary degree, the gift of inspiring others. They were impatient, and regarded discretion in their advisers as timidity or obstruction.

The widely different fortunes and circumstances of the two nations gave rise also to errors of interpretation and emphasis in the calculations of their two leaders. Winston Churchill believed that Britain was in dire and immediate peril. He spoke of fighting – he meant street fighting – '. . . if London be a heap of ashes' and the Chiefs of the Army and Air Force echoed these views and made their dispositions on the assumption of an imminent invasion. The Navy took a slightly longer view (or so the fleet dispersal would seem to indicate), but this may have been accidental.

Hitler, on the other hand, regarded the total subjection of the United Kingdom as having a fairly low priority. It was something about which he retained grave strategic misgivings.

The Fuehrer was now thinking globally. Effectively there

were, besides Germany, only four remaining military powers – the United States, Japan, Britain and Russia. Of these, the first two were remote and neutral; Britain was on the point of defeat; and Russia, the potential enemy, was the goal at which Germany's new global strategy had to be directed.

Anyone who has read *Mein Kampf* or Hitler's *Table Talk* will know his curious, split-level attitude to the English. The Fuehrer alternated between remorse and exultation at being the instrument of their destruction. Hitler's admiration for British colonial prowess and for the Indian Empire was very real. He felt a deep racial unease over taking action that would lead this whole edifice to collapse. There was also the powerful strategic argument that unless the Royal Navy and the Far Eastern garrisons were kept in being the Japanese would move in and help themselves to the rich natural resources of the East Indies.

Hitler had already given signs of reluctance to finish off the British in his peace offer after the fall of France. And yet Hitler had fought in the trenches in the First World War. Although he was only a corporal, his gallantry had earned him an Iron Cross. After the Armistice he had drifted rootlessly in Germany and seen the anguish of families starving under the blockade. It was always the British who thwarted the victorious armies of Europe – had not the Czarist and French Armies been shattered by Germany at the outset? To an astonished Rauschning in his first heady days as Chancellor, Hitler had confided: 'I will succeed where Napoleon failed. I will land on the shores of Britain.'

If the Fuehrer had strategic doubts they were amply reinforced by the tactical misgivings of several of his most senior officers (misgivings, it may be suggested, not untinged with reflection on the personal consequences of failure). Most sceptical was Grand Admiral Raeder, a sternly realistic professional who had laid the ground work for Germany's naval rearmament after Versailles and who, like all professional naval officers, regardless of country, had been schooled, even if subconsciously, to regard the British Navy as the ultimate.

Raeder's background was that of the old Imperial Navy, of that rigid discipline and spartan training whose gunnery shattered Beatty's battlecruisers at Jutland. He was the last senior officer in the Navy still to affect a wing collar with his day uniform, and had played a significant part in the expulsion of Reinhard Heydrich from the Service on account of his sexual activities. The fact that Heydrich had risen to be Himmler's Deputy in the SS, and that he made small secret of his comprehensive dossier on senior officers in the Services who had an Imperial background, did not improve Raeder's relationship with the Nazi Party. In the opening days of the Norwegian campaign the German Navy lost nearly three-quarters of its surface strength.

Now Raeder was faced with the prospect of mounting a head-on assault across open seas against the strongest naval power in the world. If it failed – regardless of the outcome of the war – the German Navy would be reduced to merely ceremonial duties. The construction programme would take at least four years to compensate. In the meantime the Naval Officers would be little more than a yacht-borne SS.

In the Army, too, enthusiasm was muted. After the Battle of France the batons had been distributed. The date, July 19, was also the occasion of Hitler's peace appeal to Great Britain. Von Manstein sourly commented that 'Hitler's appointment of a dozen Field Marshals and one Grand Admiral simultaneously was bound to detract from the prestige of a rank which had previously been considered the most distinguished in Germany'. For the New Field Marshals the risks of a cross-Channel operation must have seemed out of all proportion to the possibilities of personal advancement and glory. And these considerations can be seen reflected in the German planning. Faced with something for which they had never been trained, which had never been rehearsed in 'War Games', the staff bent over backwards to cover every possible contingency: as much to protect their own reputations and that of their commanders, it may be suggested, as to ensure the defeat of the enemy.

In fact, all the German estimates of British strength seem to have been grossly pessimistic. The very scale on which they had depleted the British reserves of equipment at Dunkirk seems to have confirmed the belief that this represented only a proportion, probably less than half, of the total available. But, if the German leadership was somewhat cumbersome and hesitant, that of the British land forces was incompetent to a frightening degree.

Montgomery has described how after his return from Dunkirk he called on General Sir John Dill, Chief of Imperial General Staff (soon to be replaced by Alan Brooke), and found him very despondent. Dill said: 'Do you realise that for the first time in one thousand years this country is now in danger of invasion?' Montgomery laughed. This did not improve Dill's temper, and he asked his subordinate what there was to laugh about. Montgomery, with characteristic candour, said that '. . . the people of England would never believe we were in danger of being invaded when they saw useless generals in charge of some of the Home commands', and gave him some examples.

The next day Montgomery received a letter at his HQ telling him to stop saying such things as it '. . . could only cause loss of confidence'.

Military thinking in the British Army was divided into two schools. The first still thought positionally and was concerned with an endless network of pill boxes and anti-tank ditches. The second school consisted entirely of the younger and more energetic officers who had served with the BEF, looked to Alan Brooke as their chief, and thought primarily in terms of mobility and rapid, concentrated counter-attacks.

Montgomery was soon kicked upstairs to command V Corps in Dorset and Hampshire. It would be comforting to believe that V Corps was being trained as a mobile reserve for direction against an enemy bridgehead; but it seems more likely that Montgomery's posting was the result of a combination of civilian pressure and Army command politics. He recorded that '. . . in the V Corps I first served under Auchinleck. I cannot recall that we ever agreed on anything'.

Montgomery has told me how, while he was with the 3rd Division at Brighton, Churchill came down to inspect the defences. 'Ever since getting back from Dunkirk I used to ask myself, "How in hell are we going to win this war?" I just couldn't see it. But after spending the afternoon with Winston, although I couldn't see *how* we were going to do it, I knew we were jolly well going to win.'

Churchill's ideas on defence were, in a tactical sense, naive and out of date. Like virtually all those charged with the protection of the realm, he had fought in the First World War, and his military thinking and reflexes were conditioned by this. His real achievement was in his capacity for inspiring those under him. Nor was this a matter solely of personal contact with the military, of 'Action-this-Day' memoranda that showered on Heads of Departments. The strength of Churchill's personality was the prime obstacle in the path of all those appeasers who did not wish to see London – least of all Threadneedle and Leadenhall Streets – a 'heap of ashes'.

The effectiveness of Churchill's leadership and the very richness of its history has obscured the recollection, and the evidence, of that large, disparate and well-placed body of 'appeasers'. They ranged from committed Fascists like Osward Mosley, through bourgeois career politicians like Sir Samuel Hoare, to clear-sighted and rational intellects like Lloyd George or Liddell-Hart. They were not only those who had attended Ribbentrop's parties at the German Embassy before the war, who had allowed themselves a flirtation with the leading Nazis (Halifax, the Foreign Secretary, is on record as having described Goering as 'a perfect pet'). But there were many, too, who thought globally – just as Hitler himself thought – who were chiefly concerned about the Soviet Union and the long-term menace which it posed to capitalist society: those who believed that a 'deal' could be fixed with the Nazis just as German industrialists had done a deal with them. And there were those, too, who weighed the relative strengths, looked at the geography, and decided resistance was profitless.

Only Churchill was single-minded enough, and bitter enough, to surmount this. For nearly 20 years he had been in the political wilderness, reviled by the Conservative Party, concerned, it seemed, in ever more ludicrous causes ranging from India to Abdication. Among 20th-century Conservatives only Enoch Powell has aroused a comparable mixture, and intensity, of love and hate in his own party. On the morning that Churchill entered the House of Commons as Prime Minister for the first time the cheers came only from the Socialist benches. And yet within days his mastery of the place was absolute.

And as Churchill's authority waxed so those who had opposed and disliked him stepped down and confirmed their grumblings to private social occasions. Sir Henry ('Chips') Channon, the diarist, buried '. . . my best bibelot's, watches, Fabergé objects, etc. Mortimer, who dug the hole, is discreet, and he waited until all the gardeners had gone home'. A few days later he was complaining of '. . . a definite plot afoot to oust Halifax, and all the gentlemen of England, from the Government, and even from the House of Commons. Sam Hoare warned Rab of this scheme only yesterday . . .' (It should be noted that historians are less likely to agree about Channon's claims to being a gentleman than they are over the undisputed aristocratic background of Sir Alexander Cadogan, the permanent head of the Foreign Office, whose recorded views of Sir Samuel Hoare are less sympathetic – 'Dirty Dog . . . collaborator . . . potential Quisling . . .')

Meanwhile, the Germans were proceeding, somewhat ponderously, with their plans to invade an enemy whose strength they had assessed at a factor of something like ten times the real figure.

Of the senior German commanders only one, Goering, was utterly confident, and he had conceived a very special, personal idea of the blow against England. Hitler seems to have been genuinely undecided. He hardly commented at all on the preparations, even in private, and there is no record of his urging haste on the participants or displaying his usual driving force when new operations were afoot. Jodl, the Chief of Staff of the combined headquarters recorded, '. . . any attempt at invasion is an act of desperation, quite unwarranted by the situation as a whole'. Raeder remained sceptical throughout. Hardly a day went past without messages of caution or complaint passing between Naval staff and Halder, the Chief of Staff to the Army.

Halder, himself a punctilious, self-effacing man with rimless glasses like Himmler's, asked nothing better than to immerse himself in the technical details of a new plan. Soon the paper began to accumulate. But whenever Halder makes a comment in his diary it is one of gloom and resignation. Halder does not seem to have appreciated the significance of the daylight battle in the skies over Britain or of the Luftwaffe casualty returns. His assessment of the RAF's strength was based entirely on the inconvenience and disruption which were caused to his own plans by the nightly raids on the invasion barges at their moorings in Calais and Dieppe.

In this uncertain company it is hardly surprising that Goering, whose new rank of Reichsmarschall gave him seniority over all Army and Naval officers and who was the sole recipient of the Grand Cross of the Iron Cross, should have become the dominant personality. He dominated every conference which he attended, resplendent in spotless summer uniforms and carrying not only the various new decorations which had been specially promulgated to honour him, but also those Imperial Orders which had rewarded his gallantry in the dark days of 1918 when, as Major Goering, he had taken command of the decimated Richtofen circus. His following of young officers was motivated by the customary mixture of hero-worship and personal advancement, and the Luftwaffe Court exuded confidence in an atmosphere where caution and hesitancy were the norm.

The Luftwaffe had never been defeated and the short life of the British air components in France and of the sorties by Fighter Command over Dunkirk had dulled the memory (except in those pilots who had actually experienced it) of the dangerous parity in fighting skill between the Germans and the RAF pilots in their eight-gun fighters. Had this been better appreciated it is probable (though not certain) that the Luftwaffe staff might have forced certain corrections to Goering's plan. The contrast between the personalities of Dowding and Goering – the gloomy, devoutly Christian ascetic with a chess player's mind, and the bombastic and arrogant Reichsmarschall – was mirrored in the *morale* of the two Air Forces.

The German pilots were the best trained. Many of them had fought in Spain and Poland; nearly all had come through the gliding schools of Luneburg and Hanover. Unlike the Army and Navy, they had been indoctrinated from the start with the Nazi ideology in all its catechism. They believed that their equipment was the best, that their enemies were inferior beings, that the triumph of the *Herrenvolk* was pre-ordained.

But now this irresistible force was to collide with an immovable object. For the British pilots, too, had a kind of indoctrination – and one more tenacious and of longer standing, stretching back through all the cruelties and taboos of a caste system, the homosexual isolation of the minor public schools, the century-old conviction – diffidently expressed, but redolent in the King-and-Country *Boys Own Paper* – that Britain always wins the last battle.

The casual laughter and off-hand modesty of the British fighter pilots concealed a combat arrogance no less total than that of their adversaries – and one more likely to endure the stresses of a long battle of attrition. As it was, the notion of gaining air supremacy by dint of an isolated aerial war beginning weeks in advance of any supplementary operations on the ground was doomed to failure. In the end, the Germans simply wore out the Luftwaffe without gaining any tactical advantage whatever, so that by the time that the possible D days started to come up on the calendar, the likelihood of air supremacy, even temporary air supremacy in the landing zone, was more remote than it had been at the start of the battle.

Formidable though the German Invasion seemed on paper, the motivation at senior command level was of indifferent quality. An uneasy coalition of reluctant Naval staff persistently complaining and creating difficulties; an Army Planning Bureau that doubled, trebled and multiplied ten fold their material requirements and precautions; and an arrogant, independent, indoctrinated Air Arm that despised the other two services and wished to take the glory of subjecting Great Britain on its own. Only the Fuehrer's personality could have imposed discipline and co-ordination on the three services, but he seems to have referred to the subject very seldom, agreeing with an alacrity unusual for him to the various postponements on which the Navy insisted.

In fact, the Germans could probably have captured London at the end of May or the beginning of June simply by using the Parachute and Airborne Divisions in no greater strength than they did against Crete the following year. Would we have fought when London was a heap of ashes? Possibly. But on balance it is more likely that a peace formula would have been found with Lord Halifax, Sir Samuel Hoare and others of Chips Channon's 'gentlemen' friends playing their part.

# Britain's Secret Resistance Movement

## by David Pryce-Jones

General Sir Colin McVean Gubbins makes no claims. He will not write his memoirs. Over 70 and retired now, he lives in a small white-painted Buckinghamshire farmhouse. The place is as trim as he is. In spite of being near the Strategic Air Command base, it is very isolated at the end of an unmade country lane, and is in its way a hide-out, somehow suitable for the man who would have led the underground resistance in the event of a German invasion in 1940.

As Colonel Gubbins, to give him his rank at the time, he was the only Englishman to have raised a secret standing army in this kingdom since the Middle Ages. At the height of the invasion crisis Churchill was personally endorsing Colonel Gubbins and the guerilla formations he was preparing for underground resistance, the Auxiliary Units as they were called. Not very many people at all were then, or ever, in the know. The underground army has not been discussed by those who were in it, especially not by Colonel Gubbins.

A former colleague says of him, 'Hard working. A Gunner. He's the kind to get things done, and there weren't so many of them in the old peace-time army.' Even the start of Colonel Gubbin's life has a perfect John Buchanesque touch. He was born in Tokyo, where his father was a member of the Legation, a leading authority on Japan and author of standard works about it. The Gubbins side of the family were Irish, and notable breeders of horses. His mother was Scottish, a McVean from the island of Mull where Sir Colin spent a large part of his childhood.

Educated at a Yorkshire prep school and then Cheltenham, he was ready for the First World War, in which he served on the Western Front until wounded late in 1918.

Pure adventure takes over. He went to Archangel as ADC to Lord Ironside, the commander of the North Russian Expeditionary Force, and stayed there for six months. At the time he learnt Russian, a language in which he is a qualified interpreter (as also in French and Urdu), and he joined what used to be known as The Great Game. Between the wars he spent two periods doing military intelligence in the War Office. In Ireland, in 1922, he had first met a number of future associates, among them an unorthodox major in the Royal Engineers, John Holland. The Irish troubles illustrated even better than his Russian experiences how a small number of guerillas operating among a friendly population can tie down a regular force. For seven years Colonel Gubbins also served in India, partly with his regiment, partly with Intelligence.

In April, 1939, as he puts it, 'this cold hand descended on my neck.' He was shifted once and for all into the world of irregular warfare. The meagre resources for undercover operations were being tentatively grouped under MI(R), or Military Intelligence (Research). One particular element coming in was Section D, a secret department in the Foreign Office whose purpose was 'to investigate any possibility of attacking potential enemies by means other than the operations of military forces'; in plain language, subversion and sabotage in enemy-held territory. Section D was small enough to be something of a family circle, although already in its bosom was Kim Philby. Another element was the War Office department known as General Staff (Research) which was virtually the private set-up of Major Holland.

Military effort and political aims were at last being co-ordinated to try to overcome bureaucratic weaknesses and rivalries. Thanks to Holland, Colonel Gubbins now took charge of the military side. 'The proverbial two men and a boy, last-minute stuff,' in the words of a colleague.

Urgently two or three courses were started in London for specially selected people not in the army but likely to be useful in a tight corner; explorers, climbers, men who knew foreign languages, and who had far-ranging business connections. Fifteen to 20 at a time, these hand-picked few were given some double-quick elementary training in wireless procedure, small-arms and explosives. Colonel Gubbins wrote three booklets of instructions which have become standard works in their turn, as he says 'often in hands about to shoot English soldiers'.

MI(R) still hoped that warfare in Nazi-occupied countries could be prepared in advance. One has the impression that Colonel Gubbins was everywhere in demand, for not only did he go on long trips round the Balkans and up to the Baltic, but he was ordered to Warsaw, in August, 1939, reaching the city just ahead of the Germany army. He was also on the disastrous expedition to Norway.

In the second week of June, 1940, Colonel Gubbins, just landed back from Narvik, was ordered to report to the CIGS and the Vice-Chief of Staff, who had been briefed by Major Holland, and then and there they told him to organise a resistance network in this country. After Dunkirk a German invasion had become an imminent likelihood. England lay more or less defenceless and unequipped – there were scarcely 200 anti-tank guns in the arsenals, with about twice that number of tanks. How exactly had the CIGS put it? 'Just get on with the job right now, they said.'

Section D had in fact already been dumping arms in various places throughout the country, but no co-ordinated scheme existed, there was no body of properly trained men, no instructors in weaponry. The only real initiative to date had been taken by General Andrew Thorne of XII Corps, whose command included the south coast from Greenwich to Hayling Island in Hampshire. At his request the War Office, sent him Peter Fleming, brother of Ian and famous already for his adventures and journeys around the world, in order to organise 'stay-behind parties' in Kent and Sussex. In the event of a German bridgehead being established within XII Corps areas, these 'stay-behind parties' were to come into action.

Peter Fleming set up his headquarters in a farmhouse called The Garth within sight of the Maidstone-Canterbury road, but with a quick retreat into wooded hills behind. His staff of about ten included Michael Calvert, later a counter-insurgency expert. Civilian helpers were soon being recruited. Preparations for laying mines and demolition charges began, and some targets like bridges were actually wired. The first regional training centre had got under way. (In *Invasion* 1940, published in 1957, Peter Fleming gave the first description in print of the resistance, though with a reticence and personal modesty which still shrouds the subject.)

Meanwhile a few rooms in 7 Whitehall Place were temporarily provided for Colonel Gubbins. 'I grabbed a few officers who had been with me in Poland and Norway, good chaps.' To begin with, he divided the whole South Coast into sectors and assigned one of his officers to each of them for the purpose of setting up a regional training centre. What Peter Fleming had already achieved was taken into the scheme.

Lord Ironside, the Commander-in-Chief of the Home Forces, put at his disposal the Intelligence forecasts of German intentions, 'for what they were worth' as Sir Colin says deprecatingly. Diversionary or even large-scale landings on any part of the coastline had to be reckoned on.

Colonel Gubbins made preliminary contact with the 12 Regional Commissioners who had been appointed by the government to run their parts of the country in the event of general collapse; with Chief Constables, with senior officers in retirement, with the local establishment. Each officer in 7 Whitehall Place was clearly going to turn to men he knew or could depend on absolutely in the sector where he was responsible for a training centre – a process which was to devolve all the way down to the grass roots in the usual English old-boy style. Colonel Gubbins obtained authority from the War Office to visit infantry depots and draw, indeed press-gang, selected personnel, though they were returned to their units 'once there was a real war', as one officer has it.

The polar explorer Andrew Croft had been on one of Colonel Gubbins's crash courses in London the previous year, and he was asked to set up the training centre and resistance organisation in his home county of Essex, much as Peter Fleming had done already in Kent and Sussex. His base was his father's house in Kelveden. In the South West, Stuart Edmundson, a Plymouth businessman, was chosen for the same task.

Leaders like these were the only men to know the names of everyone eventually enrolled in their regions – names were not recorded on paper. They in turn had to appoint subordinates to form local cells, which ideally were to consist of a commander and some five or six men. For the sake of security, each cell operated independently and had its own description as an Auxiliary Unit, a label which was carefully vague and nondescript. So much so, indeed, that rumours persist of men thinking they were being called upon for some branch of the social services.

Each man was armed with a revolver and a Fairbairn commando knife, while the cell was also allotted a tommy gun, two rifles, hand grenades and plastic explosives, then newly introduced and a great improvement on the standard gelignite. In fact the equipping of the Auxiliary Units seems to have been one of the more efficient sides of the operation, probably at the expense of the regular army. 'One morning on my doorstep were a lot of sandbags loaded with supplies,' according to one of the cell-leaders, 'I just had to stash them away'.

Nationally all Auxiliary Units were grouped into three Home Guard battalions known as 201, which was south of the Thames, 202 north of the Thames, and 203 in Scotland. Each battalion had a headquarters – 202, for example, was at Earls Colne in Essex, and later in Witham – as well as an intelligence centre. In spite of their numberings, these battalions were of course quite separate from the Home Guard, and were simply making use of a convenient cover; a deception which was Colonel Gubbins's idea. Though civilians and unpaid, the recruits did eventually receive Home Guard uniforms, mostly without formal designations, and as they were therefore not enrolled in official military units they were outside the rules of the Geneva Convention, and would have been shot out of hand on capture.

Indeed, the moment mysterious little groups of men began to muster in the countryside in the evenings, to be seen digging after dark or making inexplicable explosions, the Home Guard became suspicious. Stuart Edmundson is supposed to have told a full general to mind his own business. Resistance leaders had to be given special passes as well as identity cards, to state that 'No questions will be answered by this officer'.

'It was a bit of a shambles', one patrol leader is willing to admit, 'hush hush was something new then.' The Auxiliary Units were to spend the summer and autumn of 1941 preparing underground bunkers, three to four hundred of them, ringing the country (with the exception of the North West, where the Germans could hardly land) and complete with arms and supplies. Great ingenuity was used to conceal these places in woods, in abandoned dumps or outhouses, tunnels, behind false walls and trapdoors, even in one enlarged badger's sett.

To this day a tree stump survives where Peter Fleming devised it, at King's Wood above The Garth, which can be swung open on a hinge to reveal the entrance to a concreted emplacement below. Some of the contractors who built these places must have been mightily puzzled by their task, though sometimes the auxiliaries themselves constructed their own hideouts.

A typical example was at Little Leighs, a hamlet in Essex, where a fruit farmer called Keith Seabrook says he 'was pounced upon, recruited and told to "organise a patrol" '. They set about digging out the bottom of an old tree girt hole known as 'The Devil's Pit'. Then, working entirely at night, they built a Nissen Hut in the bottom. Twice, when they covered it with earth, it collapsed. Finally it was successfully finished, invisible, and reached by a concealed trapdoor entrance. It would have been their base for sabotage behind the German lines. The plan was hardly the blueprint for a long life. Seabrook, then a lean 27-year-old, remains coolly detached about the dangers. 'We were regarded as completely expendable. It was a three week existence. At the time I never counted the consequences.' By 1944, he controlled 70 Auxiliary patrols from Cromer to Southend, including ones in local factories, like Marconi's at Chelmsford. Throughout he went on running his fruit farm, with a plan for the immediate evacuation of his family always ready.

Bunkers were designed to be lived in by an entire cell, and were provided with food for 20 days, and with fuel for the Tilley lamps. Also with a sniper's rifle with a night sight. 'Even our wives didn't know a thing about it,' and the chestnut goes the rounds in resistance circles of the woman who believed throughout the war that the two nights of the week when her husband was away without explanation were in fact spent with another woman.

Training in techniques of sabotage, ambush and subversion were hardly less of a priority than recruiting. Number 7 Whitehall Place had been limited to bureaucracy. Once the basic network of resistance existed in outline, says Sir Colin, 'I detailed one of my staff officers, Mike Henderson, a brother of Lord Faringdon, to find a headquarters outside London where we could train in seclusion'. Coleshill was chosen, on the Berkshire Downs; built by Pratt in the 17th century, it was among the most beautiful of English houses until, sadly, it was burnt down after the war. Behind it were extensive stables and quarters for grooms where nobody could easily snoop and discover what was up – and nor would the Pleydell-Bouverie sisters still living in their big house be unduly disturbed. Colonel Gubbins moved there with his officers in August and courses were held immediately. The instructors were mostly from the Welsh Guards and their standards were not always appreciated. Fifteen to 20 patrol commanders at a time would report from all over the country in a suitably undercover manner on a Friday afternoon to the Post Office in the nearby village of Highworth, where the postmistress Miss Stranks had her part to play. She would tell the men to wait while she telephoned to Coleshill for transport. Miss Stranks was also used as a foil. Awkward questions from those who had stumbled by accident on some secret of the Auxiliary Units were stalled by referring the inquirer to the Highworth Post Office, where he would be fobbed off or passed on, according to status or the postmistress's whim.

For the whole weekend the depths of the park at Coleshill shook with bangs, and shapes crawled in the night – once it appears that some monumental accident with explosives occurred, but lips are still sealed about it. Then the patrol commanders were considered trained and had to return to their home base and pass the knowledge on to their men, the assortment of gamekeepers, sportsmen, miners, boatmen, village worthies and squires whom Sir Colin likes to recall. In the end the Auxiliary Units mustered about 3,000 all told. Had the Germans invaded that crucial Battle of Britain fortnight, Sir Colin says, 'the Auxiliary Units would have been ready'. Improvised virtually from scratch, to be sure, post-Dunkirk amateurs like everyone else, but more desperate.

'I think the point is that the army had to fight to the last man. There could be no question of allowing the German military to establish themselves here, say on a line Colchester-Weymouth. What happens after that? Who's coming to England's help at such a moment? It was a fight with your back to the wall.'

Sir Colin looks me in the eye. He is a chain-smoker and he sucks boiled sweets too. 'Supposing that a parachute battalion had been dropped near Newcastle, another at Carlisle, a third round Swindon. The confusion would have been absolute. They'd have cut us in half before we'd have been able to learn what was going on. Our communications . . .' and he stops for a moment at the unpleasant memory. 'You can't be a refugee in England, there's nowhere to go.'

So would the Auxiliary Units have been effective?

'That's not the right question. They were something additional – don't forget we hadn't taken men from regular formations, but from depots. We were expendable. We were a bonus, that's all.'

The Auxiliary Units would have come into action as guerillas on immediate contact with the Germans, cutting lines, hindering supplies, picking off what targets they could. Had the Germans over-run their sectors, they would in effect have become 'stay-behind parties', with instructions to do or die. A few weeks at very best, and they would have been wiped out along with the regular forces. None of the men had any illusions about their role by then. It was appreciated – and confirmed afterwards from German sources – that resistance would have led to reprisals against civilians of the kind which terrorised Europe. 'Yes, there had to be a Cabinet decision there, there was nothing for it, we were facing total war.'

Among weapons which developed in the circumstances was the 'time pencil' which Colonel Gubbins had brought back from Poland in 1939. This was a firing device for a booby trap, activated by acid on a wire, and therefore silent, unlike other clockwork mechanisms. Later in the war it had its successes. Also the 'sticky bombs' which had to be thrown at close-range on to the armour of a tank; as well as Molotov cocktails and other home-made bombs of phosphorous and petrol.

The morning is cold and Sir Colin shoves another log on to the fire in his tidily arranged drawing room. His dog, a short-hair German pointer, sprawls about. Lady Gubbins enters to give the dog a bone to gnaw on its favourite rug in front of the fire. Lady Gubbins is Norwegian, and they were married after the war.

Not that much effort of imagination is required to connect this domestic scene with the past. Two photographs on his writing desk show Sir Colin in full rig, with his 29 decorations. Next to them is another photograph of his son by a former marriage, John, who was killed in the war. On the walls are mementoes of various underground organisations.

For by November, 1940, it was obvious that the Germans had greatly over-estimated our defensive capacities and thereby missed their unique chance of knocking us out once and for all, and Colonel Gubbins was drafted again. He was promoted Director of Operations and Training at SOE (Special Operations Executive) with full responsibility for secret missions to Western Europe, and France above all, which took him into the orbit of General de Gaulle. In 1943 he was appointed head of SOE, vanishing deeper into the obscurities of the Official Secrets Act. The stare under those bushy eyebrows gives away nothing. The personality of someone like Sir Colin is unaffected by limelight. The success of his career has lain in anonymity, and so it remains.

Another colleague from the Military Intelligence Directorate, Colonel Bill Major, succeeded him at Coleshill. The Auxiliary Units continued to organise and to improve their underground cells. Within a year they were highly proficient. Within a year too, a whole network of transmitters and receivers had also been established, with women brought in as operators. Until D-Day the Germans were expected to stage retaliatory or diversionary raids somewhere along our extended coastline, and the Auxiliary Units would have come into action.

But as one commanding officer succeeded another at Coleshill, the backroom boys who were urgently needed elsewhere gave way to more comfortable brass hats. Those Brigade of Guards officers posted to Coleshill were now the kind of men who brought their cellars with them. Tension subsided. The cells, however, continued to meet and exercise twice a week as before.

In November, 1944, the Auxiliary Units were stood down. The secret army dispersed with less fuss but more order than it had assembled. Arms disposal remained uncertain. Some cell commanders stacked weapons away in garages and lofts and even chucked them into ponds, where 20 years later they came to light amid much amazement. Various fire-arms amnesties have exposed late caches. Here and there in the countryside small boys, or lovers perhaps, may today stumble accidently into those crumbly hide-outs which have not been filled in. Nothing else is left, hardly even the hopes and fears which went into their construction.

# Weather and Sea Conditions in SE England and the Channel in September 1940

Taken from official (hitherto unpublished) Air Ministry reports at Dungeness. Tidal information from Office of Hydrographer of the Navy, Taunton.

During the crucial period of 19th to 26th September, the weather in the Channel and on the projected invasion beaches was, on the whole, good and a crossing, even by converted river barges, would have been feasible in any sea state less than 4. The favourable weather was due to the fact that a depression from Iceland heading SE for the British Isles took a turn to the NE and went over Norway instead.

The weather began to break up on the night of 27th September, with the advent of strong Northerly winds, but by 29th the anti-cyclonic conditions were re-established. Calm conditions prevailed on 11th and 12th October, followed by a depression from the Atlantic bringing more unsettled weather conditions. This was followed once again by a period of calm from 16th to 20th October, then Easterly winds, fresh at first then light, which could have greatly assisted invasion craft from the Continent. October went out with very strong (force 8) SW winds which would have completely inhibited invasion activities.

### Thursday, 19th September, 1940, Dungeness

| Time | Weather | Visibility | Wind | Force | Sea |
|------|---------|-----------|------|-------|-----|
| 0700 | Blue sky, cloudy, some squalls. | Good | W | 4-6 | 3 |
| 1300 | Cloudy, squalls | Good | WSW | 6-7 | 4 |
| 1800 | Cloudy | Good | WSW | 6 | 4 |

**High water Dover** 0021, 17.8 ft and 1234, 18.4 ft
**Low Water Dover** 0736, 0.6 ft and 1953, 0.4 ft

**General weather forecast** at noon for the next 24 hours: Moderate to fresh SW to W winds, strong at times locally on coast, occasional rain, brighter intervals with risk of local thunder later, average temperatures.

## Friday, 20th September

| Time | Weather | Visibility | Wind | Force | Sea |
|------|---------|-----------|------|-------|-----|
| 0700 | Cloudy, squalls and blue sky | Good | W | 4-6 | 3 |
| 1300 | Cloudy, squalls | Good | WSW | 6-7 | 4 |
| 1800 | Cloudy | Good | WSW | 6 | 4 |

**General weather forecast** for next 24 hours: Fresh northerly winds decreasing moderate to light tonight; winds backing and freshening tomorrow, considerable bright periods; a few showers today; fine tonight and tomorrow.

**High Water Dover** 0052, 17.6 ft and 1304, 18.2 ft
**Low Water Dover**   0801,  0.9 ft and 2017, 1.1 ft

## Saturday, 21st September

| Time | Weather | Visibility | Wind | Force | Sea |
|------|---------|-----------|------|-------|-----|
| 0700 | Overcast, continuous drizzle | Poor | W | 1 | 1 |
| 1300 | Overcast | Poor | NE | 2 | 2 |
| 1800 | Cloudy | Good | Calm | – | 0 |

**High Water Dover** 0122, 17.4 ft and 1332, 17.6 ft
**Low Water Dover**   0831,  1.6 ft and 2044, 1.7 ft

**General weather forecast** from noon for the next 24 hours: Light NE variable winds, becoming moderate SE; rain, then a fairer interval, followed by more rain, local fog night and morning; average temperatures.

## Sunday, 22nd September

| Time | Weather | Visibility | Wind | Force | Sea |
|------|---------|-----------|------|-------|-----|
| 0700 | Cloudy | Good | S | 2 | 1 |
| 1300 | Cloudy | Good | SSW | 4 | 3 |
| 1800 | Cloudy, heavy rain | Mod | SW | 4 | 3 |

**High Water Dover** 0152, 16.9 ft and 1402, 16.8 ft
**Low Water Dover**   0856,  2.0 ft and 2112, 2.5 ft

**General weather forecast** from noon for the next 24 hours: Light to moderate southerly winds, becoming cloudy or dull; a period of rain or drizzle, spreading from SW today; local fog near S. Coast; becoming mild.

**Monday, 23rd September**

| Time | Weather | Visibility | Wind | Force | Sea |
|------|---------|-----------|------|-------|-----|
| 0700 | Cloudy | Good | W | 4 | 1 |
| 1300 | Cloudy | Good | W | 4 | 3 |
| 1800 | Cloudy, blue sky | Good | WSW | 4 | 3 |

**High Water Dover** 0223, 15.9 ft and 1441, 15.6 ft
**Low Water Dover** 0926, 2.8 ft and 2147, 3.3 ft

**General weather forecast** from noon for the next 24 hours: Moderate to light westerly wind, variable later; fine; local fog in morning; average temperatures, slight ground frost locally at night.

**Tuesday, 24th September**

| Time | Weather | Visibility | Wind | Force | Sea |
|------|---------|-----------|------|-------|-----|
| 0700 | Blue sky, cloudy | Good | NW | 1 | 1 |
| 1300 | Cloudy | Good | SW | 3 | 2 |
| 1800 | Cloudy | Good | N | 2 | 2 |

**High Water Dover** 0305, 15.1 ft and 1537, 14.7 ft
**Low Water Dover** 1006, 3.6 ft and 2236, 4.2 ft

**General weather forecast** from noon for next 24 hours: Light westerly to variable winds; fair with a little local morning fog. Average day temperature, cool at night.

**Wednesday, 25th September**

| Time | Weather | Visibility | Wind | Force | Sea |
|------|---------|-----------|------|-------|-----|
| 0700 | Blue sky, cloudy, some mist | Poor | NNW | 2 | 1 |
| 1300 | Cloudy | Good | NNE | 4 | 2 |
| 1800 | Blue sky, cloudy | Good | NE | 4 | 3 |

**High Water Dover** 0412, 14.3 ft and 1707, 14.1 ft
**Low Water Dover** 1113, 4.4 ft and 2352, 4.8 ft

**General weather forecast** from noon for next 24 hours: Light or moderate northerly winds, fresh locally on East Coast. Fair, apart from scattered showers near East Coast; rather cool.

**Thursday, 26th September**

| Time | Weather | Visibility | Wind | Force | Sea |
|------|---------|------------|------|-------|-----|
| 0700 | Cloudy | Mod | N | 2 | 1 |
| 1300 | Overcast, mist | Mod | NE by E | 4 | 3 |
| 1800 | Overcast, mist | Mod | N | 4 | 3 |

**High Water Dover** 0535, 14.0 ft and 1829, 14.0 ft
**Low Water Dover** 1237, 4.6 ft

**General weather forecast** from noon for next 24 hours: Light north or north-westerly winds, mainly cloudy, brighter intervals locally. Rather cool.

**Friday, 27th September**

| Time | Weather | Visibility | Wind | Force | Sea |
|------|---------|------------|------|-------|-----|
| 0700 | Cloudy | Poor | WNW | 3 | 2 |
| 1300 | Cloudy, mist | Mod | W | 4 | 1 |
| 1800 | Overcast, cloudy, mist | Mod | WSW | 5 | 3 |

**High Water Dover** 0711, 14.6 ft and 1948, 15.2 ft
**Low Water Dover** 0127, 4.6 ft and 1413, 3.2 ft

**General weather forecast** from noon for next 24 hours: Moderate west to NW winds, fresh at times locally; cloudy, slight showers, bright intervals later; average temperatures.

**Saturday, 28th September**

| Time | Weather | Visibility | Wind | Force | Sea |
|------|---------|------------|------|-------|-----|
| 0700 | Cloudy | Good | NW | 2 | 2 |
| 1300 | Cloudy | Good | NE | 5 | 3 |
| 1800 | Cloudy, squalls | Good | NNE | 5 | 3 |

**High Water Dover** 0815, 15.7 ft and 2048, 16.2 ft
**Low Water Dover** 0255, 3.0 ft and 1526, 2.3 ft

**General weather forecast** from noon for next 24 hours: Moderate NW to W winds, fair or fine, average temperatures.